Fiona, a feisty woman with a whimsical smile and soft wrinkles around her sparkling blue eyes, was in fine form as she met with us, advising us on every detail, right down to the petals in the flower girl's basket. She'd buzzed around the shop in happy anticipation, filled with innovative ideas. Nothing new there. Everyone i̶ ̶t̶o̶w̶n̶ knew her to be the best in the business, an̶ ̶ ̶ ̶ ̶ ̶ ̶t̶ickled she'd given us so much of her ti̶ ̶ ̶ ̶ ̶ ̶ ̶ ̶nic now, because she had so little

My mind reeled ̶ ̶ ̶ ̶ ̶ ̶ ̶ ̶less body was found just a f̶ ̶ ̶ ̶ ̶ ̶ ̶ a daisy one minute, dead th̶ ̶ ̶ ̶ ̶ ̶flowers wilting that fast, but. ̶ ̶ ̶ ̶ ̶ ̶ ̶s away at a funeral home while ma̶ ̶ ̶ ̶ ̶ ̶ no less. Convenient, but ironic.

Pushing Up Daisies

A Bridal Mayhem Mystery

Janice Hanna

HEARTSONG
PRESENTS

MYSTERIES

Dedication
In memory of my sister, Karen Doughten, who flew into the arms of Jesus last spring at the tender age of forty-five—just three days before my daughter's wedding. Many of Annie Peterson's struggles in this story are based on the anxieties I faced after losing someone I loved at such a young age.

Special Thanks
To my editor, Susan Downs.
Thanks for believing in Annie. . .and in me.

As for man, his days are like grass,
he flourishes like a flower of the field.
PSALM 103:15

ISBN 978-1-59789-761-7

Cover design: Kirk DouPonce, DogEared Design
Cover illustration: Jody Williams

Our mission is to publish and distribute inspirational products offering exceptional value and biblical encouragement to the masses.

Printed in the U.S.A.

DAISY, DAISY, GIVE ME YOUR ANSWER, DO

My daughter's love for gerbera daisies died the same day her wedding florist did. I don't think she'll ever look at flowers the same way again. I know I won't.

We received the news of Fiona Kelly's untimely demise just six hours after leaving her shop, Flowers by Fiona. My daughter Candy had finalized her wedding order that gorgeous May morning, settling on a colorful array of gerbera daisies for her big day, just four and a half weeks away. I'd written "the big check," something I'd secretly been dreading. Fresh flowers can take quite a chunk out of a wedding budget, no question about that.

Fiona, a feisty woman with a whimsical smile and soft wrinkles around her sparkling blue eyes, was in fine form as she met with us, advising us on every detail, right down to the petals in the flower girl's basket. She'd buzzed around the shop in happy anticipation, filled with innovative ideas. Nothing new there. Everyone in town knew her to be the best in the business, and we were tickled she'd given us so much of her time. It seemed ironic now, because she had so little of it left to give.

My mind reeled at the fact that her lifeless body was found just a few hours later. Fresh as a daisy one minute, dead the next. I'd heard of flowers wilting that fast, but. . .a florist? And to pass away at a funeral home while making a delivery, no less. Convenient, but ironic.

News, especially big news, travels fast in our little town of Clarksborough, Pennsylvania. Fiona's assistant, Maggie Preston, telephoned the receptionist at our local community church, my particular house of worship. She, in turn, called the pastor's wife, Evelyn. Naturally, Evelyn called Diedre Caine, who had recently taken over the e-mail prayer loop. Diedre, my daughter's future mother-in-law, happened to be related to Fiona— second cousins twice removed—so she took the news especially hard.

According to Diedre, who choked back tears as she gave me the details by phone, Fiona appeared to have died from a heart attack.

A heart attack? I thought perhaps I'd misunderstood Diedre, whose lyrical brogue often muddied the waters. How could Fiona, a woman in such fine shape, pass away so unexpectedly, with no warning at all?

"I just don't understand it, Annie." Diedre's emotion intensified as she shared her thoughts on what had happened. "Fiona was as fit as a fiddle."

Immediately my crime-fighting antennae began to rise. Call it a hunch. Call it inspiration from on high. I hung up the phone with the strongest impression that there was more to this story than met the eye. Yes, I certainly knew foul play when I smelled it, and Fiona's sudden death smelled like anything *but* a daisy.

A shiver ran down my spine as I contemplated the possibilities. Had someone taken her life out of spite, perhaps? Vengeance over a flower transaction gone awry? Had her associate done her in to steal the shop?

Had a rival florist wanted to sabotage her business? If so, how had they plotted the crime to make her death look like natural causes?

A half dozen scenarios played out in my mind, none of them making much sense. I shook off the urge to dig deeper, reminding myself that I didn't have the time to figure this out right now. Not with a wedding to plan.

So what if folks in Clarksborough saw me as something of a sleuth? Did that mean I had to get to the bottom of everything that smelled suspicious? Sure, I'd solved a crime or two over the past year. My husband, Warren, called me a lightning rod, said that trouble knew just where to strike. But I was in way over my head here, which meant I needed help—and quick.

Picking up the phone, I punched in the number for my best friend, Sheila. Menopausal and loaded with moxie, she would surely know just what to do.

Sheila answered on the first ring, her voice teeming with nervous energy. "Annie, what took you so long? I've put on ten pounds waiting for you to call." She dove into a play-by-play of all of the chocolate she'd consumed over the past half hour as she'd waited by the phone. Finally, she shifted gears. "So, what are you thinking? Looks suspicious to you, too, right?"

"I'll admit I've got a lot of questions, but I really don't think—"

"I'm sure you're like a hound dog with its nose to the ground."

I would have taken the time to scold her for such an unflattering comment, had it not been for my two mini dachshunds, who stood at the back door whimpering.

They looked up at me with woeful expressions, their beautiful brown eyes capturing my heart as always.

"Hang on, Sheila. Sasha and Copper need to go out." I fumbled with the lock, finally wriggling it loose. The anxious pups bounded onto the back porch then out into the yard, heading straight for the back of the lot. I closed my eyes and braced myself for the inevitable.

From the other side of the fence, my new neighbor's feisty Maltese started a high-pitched barking fit, and within seconds, my two pups joined in. On and on the yap-fest went, making it nearly impossible to focus on my phone call. I watched out of the corner of my eye as Copper, the newest addition to our family, pounced on the fence, trying to knock it down. I shuddered—in part because Warren had just repaired it last week and in part because the Maltese had managed to sneak into our yard once already.

Copper tended to run a little on the territorial side. Thank goodness he weighed in at less than fifteen pounds. Any bigger and he might actually be dangerous, and not just to a feisty little Maltese.

Sheila, never one to be upstaged, kept talking through all the barking, and I struggled to make out her words. After the dogs settled down, I finally heard the tail end of her conversation—pun intended.

"Annie, I know you." The excitement in her voice picked up. "You have a God-given gift for snooping."

"Excuse me?"

"You know what I mean. You're great at figuring things out."

I knew better than to argue with her, of course,

especially when I'd already felt the tug on my heart to investigate. How could I not, with Fiona's death so closely tied to my daughter's big day? And yet how could I take the time to play this hunch now, with wedding plans consuming my life?

"This whole thing about Fiona has me worked up." Sheila spoke with great passion. "She was such a wonderful woman. Never hurt a flea. And if she didn't die of natural causes, if someone murdered her, then we've got a killer on the loose. I can't help but wonder who will be next."

"Stay calm, Sheila."

"This *is* calm," she interjected. "Trust me, I could be far more worked up. Point is, we can't just sit around and wait for an autopsy report. That could take weeks. We've got to do something, if for no other reason than to put our minds at ease."

"Well, let's get together and see what we can come up with."

"W.O.W. starts in an hour," she reminded me. "Can you come up to the church a little early so we can talk? We'll have to wrap up quick though, because tonight's the big night."

"Ah." I'd forgotten. Our beloved pastor's wife had cooked up some sort of scheme for our Women of the Word Bible study group. A big surprise, details to be revealed this evening at our weekly meeting. I wasn't really in the mood for any more surprises but had promised to attend after Evelyn put a little bug in my ear that tonight's meeting somehow involved Candy's wedding.

"I'll meet you there," I agreed. "But Sheila, before

we do anything else, let's pray about this. The last thing I need to do is add one more thing to my ever-growing list. And besides, if the police don't suspect foul play, it's likely that Fiona died of natural causes, just like they said."

"Humph."

I ended the call, determined to give the matter to the Lord one way or another. If anyone had the answer to the "What happened to Fiona Kelly?" question, He did.

WHERE HAVE ALL THE FLOWERS GONE?

A half hour after talking to Sheila, I arrived at the church, husband and son in tow. Warren gave me a kiss on the cheek and headed off to make the coffee for the men's group. Devin, our eighteen-year-old, made his way to the gym with guitar in hand for worship team practice.

I located Sheila in the fellowship hall gabbing with Evelyn. I tried not to sigh aloud as I looked at our beautiful pastor's wife but found it difficult. Though considerably older than me, Evelyn was in excellent shape. Why, everything about the woman reeked of perfection. Even if I spent months at the gym, my upper arms would never look like hers. No, mine preferred to wave in the breeze while hers appeared to be wrapped in tight layers of plastic wrap.

And Sheila. . .what could be said about such an eclectic individual? I smiled as I noticed her new hairdo. The shorter style threw me a little. I'd never witnessed Sheila with spiky hair before. Had Candy, in her zeal as a new stylist at our local salon, talked my best friend into this new look? Surely not.

I contemplated Sheila's many changes over the years. Like a chameleon, she transformed to suit every mood or season. You never knew what you were going to get with her. On the other hand, her hair looked pretty cool with those new lime green capris and that hot pink blouse. The bright jewelry added the extra-special touch that made Sheila. . .Sheila. Still, I had to wonder how her husband felt about the fact that he'd married so many different women.

She stood as I entered the room and ushered me to a far corner so we could have some privacy. "You can wait to compliment my new 'do' later." Sheila winked. "Though, personally, I think Candy is the best stylist ever to be hired on at The Liberty Belle. But first, tell me every detail of your meeting with Fiona earlier today so we can get to work." She flipped open a notebook and reached into her purse for a pencil.

"Wow. You're really taking this seriously."

"Of course. It's your influence." She gave me a pensive look then started asking the usual who, what, when, where, and why questions. Minutes later, I'd taken over control of the sleuthing notebook and had written down the facts as we saw them:

> WHO: Fiona Kelly was a well-loved and respected business owner in Clarksborough with no known enemies.
>
> WHAT: An unexpected death. Police suspect a heart attack.
>
> WHEN: Wednesday afternoon, approximately 3:00 p.m.
>
> WHERE: Fiona's body was discovered at Moyer's Funeral Home in the nearby town of Wallop, approximately fifteen miles from her place of business.
>
> WHY?

We decided to leave the WHY? slot empty for now, though one idea came to mind right away.

"Do you think Maggie had something to do with this?" I whispered. After all, Fiona's assistant had been the one to call the church. "Maggie's been acting mighty strange lately, hasn't she? I've heard more than one person say she's been really short with them. Rude, even. That's not like her."

"And I have it on good authority that she's cut way back on her hours," Sheila added. "I've been by the shop a couple of times over the past week or so, and she wasn't there. Maybe she and Fiona had some sort of disagreement."

"But over what?" I asked. "Something to do with the shop?"

"Likely, though I don't recall ever seeing them argue." Sheila's eyes widened. "But it would make sense. Fiona didn't have any children of her own, and she always treated Maggie like a daughter, so she probably did plan to leave the shop to her."

"Makes me wonder if Fiona had a will," I added. "And if Maggie's in it." I pondered that for a moment then pushed the idea aside. "Still, it's too obvious. And how—or why—would Fiona pass away at the funeral home instead of the flower shop?"

Sheila shrugged, then her eyes lit with a revelation. "Maybe Maggie has been slowly poisoning Fiona for months. Putting arsenic in her coffee or something like that." She dove into a story about a television show she'd seen with a similar scenario, but I felt compelled to interrupt.

"Sheila, that doesn't make sense. People with heavy

metal poisoning show signs of illness for months before they pass away. Whoever murdered Fiona Kelly must've used a poison that killed her instantly. Not that there are a lot of ingestible poisons that work that fast. If, in fact, she was poisoned at all. I'm still not convinced. Maybe we're getting all worked up over nothing."

Feeling a tap on my shoulder, I turned to face my twin daughters, Brandi and Candy. I smiled as I looked into their beautiful faces.

Candy pressed a strand of long brown hair behind her ear as she sat down next to me. "Mom, did you hear the news? I can't believe we were just with Fiona a few hours ago and now. . ."

"Now she's gone," Brandi whispered. "It's so hard to believe. You know how health conscious she was. Something about all of this just feels wrong. Suspicious."

"Brandi, don't even go there." Candy turned to her with a frown then directed her next words at me. "If Mom thinks Fiona's been murdered, she'll try to figure out who did it, and right now I need her to stay focused on the wedding plans. We're down to the last few weeks, you know."

Swallowing hard, I pushed the sleuthing notebook back toward Sheila, who managed a strained cough.

"What?" Candy gave me an accusing look. "What's going on with you two? What are you up to?"

"Oh, nothing." I offered up an innocent shrug. "Just chatting."

"About. . . ?" Brandi gave me a pensive look.

"Just stuff."

Brandi snatched the notebook and opened it, reading aloud. I cringed at the look on Candy's face.

"Mom, tell me you're not getting involved in this. Remember what happened last time?" She reminded everyone within hearing distance that my last two crime-solving escapades had interrupted Brandi's wedding plans. As she wrapped up the story, she crossed her arms at her chest and stared me down. "And besides, Fiona Kelly died of natural causes."

I mouthed "Please be quiet" and forced a smile as several of the women looked our way.

Candy groaned. "I told Garrett this was going to happen."

Thankfully, a voice rang out from across the room, interrupting our conversation. I looked up to see Evelyn clapping her hands. "Ladies, could I have your attention, please?"

We rose from our seats and made our way to where the others were gathered. Candy chose the spot next to Diedre. *Great. Now she's picking her future mother-in-law over me.* Just as quickly, I chided myself. Diedre had, after all, lost a family member this afternoon. And Candy had never given me any reason to doubt her love. No point in crying over milk that hadn't even spilled yet.

Evelyn gave us a motherly smile as she kicked off the meeting. "I'm glad you could make it." Her eyes brimmed over as she continued. "I'm sure you've all heard the news about Fiona."

Voices began to layer on top of one another as the women talked about our beloved local florist and her unexpected death.

Evelyn's expression shifted from compassion to joy as she continued. "Diedre and I have been cooking up an idea we think you're all going to love. One that was inspired by Candy Peterson's upcoming wedding and one, ironically, that can be used as a tribute to Fiona's love of flowers."

I looked at my girls for reassurance. Whatever these ladies had up their sleeves had something to do with my daughter, and anything having to do with one of my children ultimately had something to do with me.

"For months I've wanted our W.O.W. group to do a Bible study focused on the Proverbs 31 woman," Evelyn explained.

I couldn't help the groan that escaped. There were at least a dozen other biblical heroines I'd rather study than the Proverbs 31 woman. That "practically perfect in every way" gal always managed to put me to shame. Kind of like Evelyn. Who could keep up with someone who rose before dawn to care for her family, sold her wares to the local merchants for a profit, planted vineyards, and still had time left over to clothe her household in scarlet? Not me, even on my best day. I had enough trouble keeping up with my editing clients and the never-ending wedding plans. And my son's upcoming graduation. And the occasional crime-solving venture, of course.

Evelyn continued on, oblivious to my ponderings. "Candy will be married in the sanctuary on the first Saturday afternoon in June and will hold her reception in the courtyard afterward. It's going to be a summertime garden party with hors d'oeuvres, finger sandwiches, and a lovely three-tiered cake topped with daisies. As you know, we've been working to clear out that area during the past few weeks, and it will be ready for landscaping soon." She shared her vision of how beautiful the area would be with a little work.

"So, here's our idea. . . ." Evelyn turned to Diedre, who offered an encouraging smile. "We're going to plant a vineyard, just like the Proverbs 31 woman."

Sheila raised her hand, and I took note of the perplexed look on her face as she posed her question. "Is that your fancy way of saying *we're* going to do the landscaping?"

"Yes." Evelyn clasped her hands together and smiled, clearly delighted with the idea. "But here's the best part. All the while we'll be studying the Proverbs 31 woman, specifically the part of the story where she plants a vineyard. We'll also examine scriptures from the New Testament about planting and reaping to see what the Lord has to say on the subject. We're going to learn as we go. . .about life, gardening, and womanhood."

Another groan escaped my lips. I didn't even try to stop it. Gardening and womanhood? Was she kidding?

"Our Bible study will be divided into sections that correspond with our work in the garden," Evelyn explained. "The project will begin next Wednesday afternoon, and our scripture for the first lesson is from Proverbs 31:16: 'She considers a field and buys it; out of her earnings she plants a vineyard.' Because Candy is featuring gerbera daisies at her wedding, we'll plant several of those as well as a host of other colorful flowers—sunflowers, zinnias, marigolds, and more. But first we'll learn to prepare the soil, add the nutrients, and so forth. What do you think?"

"Fabulous idea!" one of the older women interjected.

"Fabulous, my eye," Sheila whispered. "I just got a manicure this morning. Can you see these hands digging in the dirt?" She held out her shiny pink nails for my examination then withdrew them with a sigh. "Why don't we just hire landscapers, like every other church in town? I'd be happy to pitch in to pay for it."

She started to raise her hand, but I snatched it before she could do so. "Sheila, they're doing this out of love for my daughter and out of respect for Fiona."

"Humph."

Evelyn kept talking, but I barely heard a word. Only when Diedre stood and made her way to the front of the room did I snap back to attention. She brushed away a tear as she spoke in her beautiful Irish brogue. "In light of what has happened, we have decided to dedicate the garden to our beloved Fiona. As most of you know, she was my second cousin twice removed."

A hum filled the room as the women took to chatting among themselves.

"Fiona was a wonderful teacher and taught me so much about gardening over the years. I want to pass on what I've learned. With that in mind, I'm going to lead you through the process of planting a flower garden from a biblical perspective, everything from tilling the ground to planting the seeds to reaping a harvest. Each step of the way we will study the parallels between the garden and our own spiritual walk, tying it all back to the Proverbs 31 woman."

Okay, so I had to admit that sounded pretty interesting. Clever, even. I looked at my daughter's future mother-in-law, a little unnerved. I hated to think she possessed qualities I did not—qualities Candy would learn to admire and even emulate. If Diedre

Caine could dig in the dirt. . .if she could discover her womanhood crawling around on her knees in a manure-filled bed of daisies. . .well, so could I.

Maybe.

Diedre continued on. "I've titled the first lesson, 'Consider a Field,' taking my cues from the Proverbs 31 woman."

"This sounds like so much fun!" Janetta Mullins, Clarksborough's caterer extraordinaire, spoke up from the row behind me. "And I'll be happy to bring the snacks for our meetings. What do you think of this idea? Each week we'll eat foods found in a garden."

"Terrific," Sheila whispered in my ear. "Not only are we going to ruin our nails, we're going to overdose on broccoli and cauliflower and develop an addiction to dandelion tea."

I couldn't help the giggle that escaped as I envisioned Janetta Mullins passing around trays of cucumber sandwiches and carrot sticks.

Candy looked my way with a "Mom, you're disturbing the meeting" look, and I did my best to calm down. When did my girls become the mother?

Leaning back in my chair, my thoughts shifted from gardening to Fiona, the woman who'd always had the greenest thumb in town. I remembered the sparkle in her eyes. Contemplated the joy in her expression. Balanced all of that against Evelyn and Diedre's plan to plant a garden in her honor.

Had Fiona really died from natural causes, or had someone taken her life? How would I ever know if I didn't get involved?

With new resolve, I decided to just that. . .and the sooner, the better.

3

FLOWER DRUM SONG

I sometimes wonder which is tougher. . .solving crimes or living with pets.

Strike that. Murder is nothing compared to a duo of disobedient dachshunds.

On Thursday morning I awoke to the oddest noise—kind of a chomping, grinding sound. I nudged Warren, who let out a sleepy groan.

"What is it, Annie?" He rolled over and looked at me, eyes filled with concern.

"Do you hear that?" I whispered.

We both lay in silence for a few seconds, just listening. Warren eventually sat up in the bed, and Sasha, who'd been snuggled under the covers between us, came scrambling out with a low growl in the back of her throat. I did my best to shush her before calling Copper's name.

No response.

"That's strange." Usually Copper woke us bright and early with soggy kisses. I patted the comforter in the usual spot, but there was no lump. "He's gone."

The odd sound continued, and I swung my legs over the side of the bed, realization kicking in. "Oh no. Don't tell me he's. . ." I stared down at the ornery canine, who chewed the wooden leg of the bed with vigor.

Warren bounded from the bed and joined me, a look of half-awake anger on his face as he saw the evidence of the crime. He reached for the dog and I cringed. "Spanking him won't do any good," I interjected. "Dogs need positive reinforcement, not negative."

"Well, if he ever *did* anything positive, I'd reinforce him." Warren now held the pup, which began to lick him in the face. After a moment or two, the tightness in his jaw relaxed—Warren's, not the dog's—and I could tell that Copper had won him over.

"See, he's not all bad," I offered.

Warren turned to me with a sigh, and for the first time I noticed that his salt and pepper hair stood up all spiky across the top of his head. . .kind of like Sheila's.

"Annie," he admonished, "you've got to take these two monsters to obedience school, like you promised to do months ago."

"I know, I know. I've just been so busy with the weddings and Devin's graduation plans. And my clients." I wanted to add, "Who do you think I am, the Proverbs 31 woman?" but stopped myself.

After a deep sigh, I promised to swing by Coats 'n Tails, Clarksborough's premiere pet shop, later this morning. The pups needed their nails clipped anyway, and Sasha was long overdue to have hers painted. I could drop the little darlings off to be bathed and groomed, ask about obedience classes, and then make my way over to Moyer's Funeral Home for round one of questioning. Afterward I would pick up the dastardly duo.

After letting the dogs out for their usual yap-fest with the Maltese, I settled in to read my new Bible, the one the girls had given me for my birthday. I chuckled as I ran my finger across the name they'd had imprinted on the front: ANNIE PETERSON, SUPERSLEUTH. They'd joked that maybe I'd uncover some mysteries in the Word of God as I read. Ironically, this morning I had a major mystery to unearth.

Gardening. I would study up on it. See what the Lord had to say about it. And I might—*shiver*—actually read the thirty-first chapter of Proverbs. On purpose.

Just twenty minutes into my study—which, ironically, began in the Garden of Eden—the phone rang. I smiled as I glanced at the caller ID. Sheila. I knew before answering what she would say but pressed the TALK button anyway.

"Annie, what time are you picking me up?"

"Picking you up?" I played innocent.

"You're going to Moyer's Funeral Home, right? At least that's what I'd do if I were you. Start at the scene of the crime and go from there."

"You mean, 'Start where the body was located.' After all, we don't know that a crime has been committed. But, yes, Sheila, I am going to the funeral home. And I will pick you up in forty-five minutes. I've still got to get dressed and put on some makeup." I paused a moment then added, "Oh, and Sheila. . ."

"Yes?"

"Let's dress conservatively. It is a funeral home, after all. We want to be respectful."

"Con. . .servatively?" She seemed to stumble over the word. "You mean, like, darker colors? Nothing too bright?"

"Exactly."

"Um, okay. I'll be ready when you get here. You won't even recognize me."

Why didn't that surprise me?

After a quick shower, I put the dogs in the car and made my way to town. I noticed the forsythias in full bloom, and the white blossoms of the pear trees took my breath away. Why, I could think of nothing prettier than Pennsylvania in the springtime. Colorful, vibrant, radiating with life.

In the midst of my springtime reverie, I happened to pass Flowers by Fiona and noticed the CLOSED sign on the door. Hmm. Not *everything* was radiating with life, was it? No, I had to wonder if Maggie would carry on with the business. *Maggie, why aren't you at the shop? What are you up to?*

Minutes later, I pulled my car into the driveway at Sheila's house, and she bounded from the front door dressed in the craziest leopard print getup I'd ever seen. Her black boots and rhinestone studded sunglasses really topped off the ensemble. She gave me a bubbly smile and waved then sprinted in my direction.

After shooing Sasha and Copper out of the way, Sheila climbed into the passenger seat then gestured to her outfit. "I had a doozy of a time finding something in black, but I finally managed."

"Black?" Hmm. Okay, upon further examination, there did appear to be a bit of black in the fabric's vibrant print, though I had to search for it. I smiled and took a couple of deep breaths.

"So what's the deal with Mutt and Jeff here?" She gestured to the dogs, and I released an exaggerated sigh.

"I'm dropping them off at the groomer's on the way. Don't worry."

As if to somehow woo her, Copper scrambled

into Sheila's lap and began to give her slobbery kisses. Sheila groaned and pushed him away. "This dog needs therapy. Or a girlfriend."

"He has a girlfriend." I pointed at Sasha, who sat in the backseat.

"She must be falling down on the job."

"Um, not exactly." In fact, I'd witnessed just the opposite. The two had been inseparable, especially for the past couple of weeks.

Minutes later we pulled into the parking lot of Coats 'n Tails, and with Sheila's help, I managed to take the collars off both dogs, explaining that they were going to be bathed. Sheila helped, but she didn't look particularly happy about it.

No collars meant no leashes, which meant the dogs had to be carried to the door. I grabbed Copper, the larger of the two, and Sheila reluctantly took Sasha into her arms. My little darling licked her on the cheek—a gesture of kindness—but Sheila didn't seem to take well to doggie kisses.

We made it to the front door of Coats 'n Tails with both dogs. Unfortunately, we found the door locked and a sign posted in the front window.

"Closed for Renovations"? Sheila read aloud.

"You've got to be kidding me." I looked down at Copper, who stared at me with his tail wagging merrily. "So now what do we do?"

"Take them with us, I guess."

"To the funeral home?" Visions of Copper chewing the edges off a top-of-the-line mahogany casket flitted through my mind, and I shuddered all the way down to my pocketbook. "I can't imagine it."

"I have to meet Orin for lunch at noon," Sheila explained. "So that leaves me with a limited amount of time. We can take the puppies with us. It's a pretty day out. Nice and cool, too. We'll just crack the car windows when we get there. They'll be fine."

Though everything within me argued against it, I finally agreed. We set out for Wallop and arrived at Moyer's in short order. Perfectly organized rows of cars tipped us off to the fact that a funeral was taking place inside. Careful to avoid the line of graveside-bound traffic, I opted to park on the far side of the lot nearest the cemetery.

Slipping the car into park, I looked around the parking lot in amazement. "This place gets a lot of business."

Sheila shrugged. "Well, you know what they say: 'Where there's a will, there are five hundred relatives.'"

She erupted in laughter, and I couldn't help but join in. However, out of the corner of my eye, something, or rather, *someone* distracted me. I took note of the caretaker, an older fellow with curly white hair, tending to the flower garden off to our right. He seemed a bit stiff as he moved up and down. "Poor guy. I'll bet he has quite a story."

"Annie, we *all* have a story. If someone took the time to examine your life—or mine—they'd find plenty to talk about."

"True. Still. . ." For whatever reason, watching him work in the dirt like that reminded me of Evelyn and our upcoming project. Maybe this fellow could teach us a thing or two about gardening. If the courtyard at church turned out half as pretty as the landscaped area in front of me now, we'd all be happy. . .especially the bride-to-be.

Oh, how I wanted this wedding to go well for Candy and Garrett. If any two people deserved an event-free wedding, these two did. Meticulous to the last detail, they'd both worked so hard to make everything perfect for everyone. Yes, Candy would surely turn out to be the twenty-first-century version of the Proverbs 31 woman. I could just see her now, balancing her career as a hairstylist with her role of wife and mother. Her children would be immaculate and well-groomed, of course. Never a hair out of place. They would eat homegrown foods straight from the garden she and her mother-in-law labored in, side by side.

My heart grew heavy as I pondered that possibility, so I opted to focus on the wedding. My eyes filled with tears as I thought about Candy walking down the aisle toward her husband-to-be, ready to take his hand, his heart, his. . .name.

Hmm. We tried not to focus much on that part. Marrying into the Caine family wouldn't have been an issue for Brandi, but for Candy, well. . .

"Everything okay?" Sheila's voice roused me from my thoughts.

"Oh, yeah. Fine. Just thinking about the wedding." I gave the funeral home a solid once-over, knowing I needed to shift gears from weddings to funerals. Pulling the key from the ignition, I turned to Sheila. "We've got to have a reason for being here."

Her brow wrinkled as she responded, "We have a reason. We're tracking down a murderer."

"We can't just show up at a funeral home asking

questions about a murder like we're the police or something. I say we go in there and ask for information about something pertaining to, say, our own funerals."

"Ugh." The wrinkles in her brow deepened. "What do you mean?"

"I don't know. Maybe ask about prepaid funeral plans or something like that. Make it look like we're customers. And who knows. . .maybe we will be someday. This is all usable information."

Sheila grew silent, something that happened so rarely that I began to get nervous. She finally whispered, "I haven't been in a funeral home since Judy Blevins died last fall."

A chill came over me at the mention of Judy's name. It had been months since either of us had spoken of our good friend, perhaps because her death had awakened us to the possibility that life was more fragile than we'd thought. She'd died in her early fifties. Far too young, to my way of thinking, though I certainly couldn't question the Almighty or ask the "Why?" question. I wasn't sure I'd like the answer, anyway.

"I'm not sure I can do this, Annie. And if we get to talking about the price of caskets and all that. . ." Sheila's voice trailed off.

I reached over and patted her hand. "It's okay. I'll do the talking. You just keep your eyes and ears open for clues. We'll get through this. And like I said, we're going to have to face this funeral issue one day, anyway."

"Well, yeah," she muttered, "but I'd rather face it looking up from the casket, not into it. What's the point of dying if you have to make arrangements first? That's like going to a restaurant but still having to plan the meal for everyone beforehand. Is everything in life prearranged these days? Even death?" She shuddered. "Can't I just leave all the details to Orin and the kids?"

I didn't offer my thoughts on the matter, in part because they differed so greatly from hers. Why should my family members have to fight over what sort of casket to put me in or which songs to play at my service? I wanted all of that ironed out beforehand.

Which meant I'd better get busy.

I rolled the windows down about four or five inches and let out a sigh. "I sure hope the dogs will be okay."

"They'll be fine." Sheila removed her seat belt and bounded from the car. "Let's get to work, Agatha Annie."

"Mm-hmm." I exited the car and closed the door. Speaking through the opening in the window, I gave the pups a lengthy lecture about the need for peace and quiet. "There's a funeral going on, so no yapping! Play it cool."

I pointed my finger at Copper, but ironically it was Sasha who peered at me through the glass with a suspicious glint in her eye.

"I don't know about this, Sheila." Worry swept over me. "I've got a bad feeling."

"There's no turning back now. Let's just get this over with." She took off toward the front door of the funeral home, and I sprinted along behind her. Maybe if we stayed for just a few minutes the dogs would be fine.

Before stepping inside, I turned back for one last look at the car to ease my mind. Sasha's nose poked out above the window. I gave her a warning look, just in case she had any wild ideas. Then, determined to learn all I could about who had killed Fiona Kelly—and why—I entered the vestibule of Moyer's Funeral Home.

4

You Don't Bring Me Flowers

There's something about walking into a funeral home, even when you're not there for a service or viewing, that just sends a shiver down the spine.

Sheila and I entered through the heavy double doors of Moyer's, finding ourselves in a beautifully designed foyer. From above, the sound of piped-in music played a soothing melody. Directly in front of us, a somewhat mousy-looking, middle-aged woman sat at an ornate wooden desk talking on the phone. She looked up as we entered and mouthed, "Just a minute, please," and then pushed a strand of graying brunette hair behind her ear and turned her attention back to the phone.

While we waited, I took a moment to examine the area with an investigator's eye. Where had the police found Fiona's body again? I should've called Sergeant O'Henry at the Clark County sheriff's office to ask for specifics. Then again, asking for information would raise red flags. For now, I'd better stick to snooping. If I could get Sheila to cooperate. She looked a bit pale.

The foyer opened onto an oak-paneled hallway lined with oversized wooden doors on either side. I turned back to glance at the woman at the front desk to make sure she was preoccupied, whispered, "Stay right here," to Sheila, then slipped through the first door on the right.

Yikes. A viewing room. With casket. And body. I gazed down into the face of the woman about my age, and my heart lurched. I drew back and took note of the casket spray—a beautiful arrangement of red roses. Whoever she was, she had been loved, and that meant friends and family couldn't be far away. I slipped back into the hallway, bumping into the woman from the front desk who now stood next to Sheila, chatting.

"Oh, are you with the Radisson family?" she asked. "You've come a bit early. Private viewing for the family begins at noon. Public viewing at one."

"Oh, no, actually. . ."

"Could you direct us to the ladies' room?" Sheila interjected.

"Ah, I see. Yes, it's down that hall to the left. Second door." She pointed, and I headed off in that direction on Sheila's heels.

"Fast thinking on your part," I mentioned, "and trust me, I need the pit stop after what I saw in that room. I wasn't prepared for a private viewing, especially when I didn't even know the deceased." I wanted to add, "She looked younger than us," but didn't. Instead, I guided Sheila into the ladies' room for a private chat.

"Annie, I don't think I can do this." She placed a trembling hand on my arm. "You have no idea the lengths I've gone to over the past several months to avoid thinking about death."

I knew Sheila to be a woman of faith, so I took her by the hand and gazed into her fear-filled eyes. "I'm not trying to be morbid by coming to a funeral home. If you're uncomfortable, we can go."

"No." She fidgeted with her purse. "It was my idea to come in the first place. I'm just thinking that maybe I should've waited in the car with the dogs."

"We won't be long, I promise."

I entered the first stall, chattering the whole way. Something above the toilet caught my attention. *A vent. Hmm.* I filed the information away, convinced that it would come in handy.

Minutes later, Sheila and I made our way back out to the foyer. By now the funeral service had let out, and dozens of mourners flooded toward us.

"Goodness." I leaned against the wall, trying to figure out what to do as the throng of grieving people pressed in around me. An idea flitted through my mind. Why not take advantage of this opportunity? With such a crowd, no one would notice my activity, right?

"You wait right here, Sheila," I whispered. "I'm going to take a quick look around."

Sheila's bug-eyed stare told me she'd rather not, thank you, but she inched her way past the mob and sat in a plush chair in the hallway. I made my way beyond a grieving couple and rapped on the door marked DIRECTOR. Thankfully no one responded, so I opened the door and slipped inside then closed the door behind me.

Flipping on a light switch, I took in the room. Wow. Not bad. Fabulous desk and oak bookshelves, stocked with books on grieving. On the desk, alongside a calendar and pen, sat a plateful of brownies. *So, a funeral director who likes chocolate.* I almost reached out and grabbed one but thought better of it, what with my daughter's wedding coming up in a few weeks. I could practically read Sheila's mind from here: *A minute on the lips, forever on the hips.* To the right of the brownies I took note of a nameplate that read EDDIE MOYER. Must be the funeral director.

Just then the door flew open and I found myself face-to-face with a rather intimidating looking man—slightly overweight with thinning black hair—dressed in an impressive Italian suit. He took one look at me, and shock registered in his eyes. "C–can I help you?"

Wow. Deep voice. He'd chosen the right profession, no doubt about that.

"I, um, I'm a bit turned around," I started. "I was just looking for. . ."

A female voice interrupted us, and I turned to discover the woman from the front desk staring at me with wide eyes. "Mr. Moyer, I'm so sorry." She gave him an apologetic look then turned my way and directed her next words at me. "Ma'am, I believe I mentioned that the ladies' room was the *second* door on the left, not the first."

"Oh, I, uh. . ."

The director seemed to relax a bit. "It's all right, Louise, er, Miss McGillicuddy. Could've happened to anyone."

I noticed the expression in her eyes as she gazed at him. Hmm. I knew that look well. This was a woman in love. Only one problem. . . My supersleuthing abilities tipped me off to the fact that he wore a wedding ring. She did not. Clearly, they were not Mr. and Mrs.

"Can I help you with something?" Mr. Moyer took a seat and gave me a pensive look.

"Well, actually, yes. My friend Sheila and I had hoped to talk with you about prearranged funeral plans."

Sheila, never one to miss a cue, appeared in the open doorway at that very instant, a calm unassuming look on her face. The woman could've taken home an Academy Award for her smooth performance.

Eddie Moyer's face lit up as he slipped into business mode. "Well, you've come to the right place."

I extended my hand. "My name is Annie Peterson. I live in Clarksborough, and I've heard such wonderful things about Moyer's over the years." That part happened to be true. Moyer's had taken care of all of the arrangements for Judy's funeral, after all. "I had to come and see for myself."

Louise pursed her lips, as if she found me suspect. I didn't really blame her. "Would you like me to visit with them, Mr. Moyer?" she offered. "I wouldn't mind, and I know you're busy."

"No, I have time." He gestured for us to take a seat on the opposite side of his desk, and Louise scooted out of the room, looking perturbed.

"First, let me thank you for choosing Moyer's Funeral Home," he began. "I know you have other choices closer to home, so it speaks volumes that you've come to us. We've been in business since the 1930s and have walked thousands of Pennsylvania families through the process of planning for their big day."

Yikes. He made it sound like a wedding, not a funeral. And I noticed the rehearsed smile on his face. He'd been through this speech a time or two before.

Mr. Moyer reached for a packet with the words

PRE-NEED PACKAGE on the front and slipped it across the desk in my direction. "I'm a firm believer in planning ahead. When you take care of the details before you pass, you spare your family members from having to make difficult decisions. I've been in this business for years and can tell you, grieving friends and family members are hardly in the right state of mind to be making tough choices."

"Tough like which casket do we pick, the stainless steel or pine?" Sheila asked. "Or which lining do we want, satin or crepe? Because, frankly, I'd rather let someone else figure all that out."

"Oh, well, then why are you—"

I cut him off, anxious to get back into the conversation. "*I'm* shopping. She's simply here as my friend." I shot a glare her way. "My moral support."

"I see." He plastered on a stiff smile and directed his next words at me. "Well, Ms. Peterson, once you have chosen one of our plans, you can put your worries aside. Those of us at Moyer's Funeral Home will carry out your wishes in a professional manner."

"Tell me how this works."

"Of course." He opened the booklet and began to move through it as he spoke. "We have three plans available, each offering its own level of funeral arrangements. You choose based on your personal preferences. And your budget, naturally."

"Naturally." Sheila muttered something under her breath, and I gave her a gentle kick in the shins to quiet her.

"We can tailor a funeral plan to meet your exact requirements and specifications." He dove into a lengthy speech, losing me somewhere along the way as my gaze shifted once again to the plate of brownies. He pushed them my way, pausing to smile. "Go ahead, take one. Be my guest."

I thought at once of my dimpled thighs. "Um, no thank you. I'm watching my waistline."

He chuckled as he pulled the plate back across the desk to its original spot. "Yeah, me, too. And it's getting easier to watch every day, which is why my new wife has me on a diet."

New wife?

He sighed. "I haven't touched these, but I hate to hurt Louise, um, Miss McGillicuddy's, feelings. She used to bring homemade brownies every Wednesday . . .until I got married a few months back. Then she stopped." He glanced down at the plate and chuckled. "Started up again this week, though. Must've heard the news that Gloria's got me on a diet."

"Oh?" My curiosity got the better of me.

He shrugged. "Must be trying to tempt me. I never could resist Louise's brownies, but I don't need the sugar."

We spent a few more minutes talking about dieting—a subject I knew well—and then I shifted the conversation back to business. At one point, something behind Mr. Moyer caught my attention: a vent on the wall behind the desk. *Hmm.* Was it somehow connected to the one in the ladies' room? My thoughts shifted in several different directions at once as I thought about the possibilities. Yes, indeed. This would come in handy for future snooping.

By the time the clock struck eleven, we'd talked

through all my options and I'd promised to return with a decision. Soon. What would it hurt? Warren and I often talked about this very thing.

Eddie Moyer ushered us out into the hallway, where we found Louise engaged in a heated phone call at the front desk. Though I didn't deliberately listen in, I couldn't help but hear a few words coming from her end.

"Mr. Kratz, we've been over this several times." She spoke with great passion. "And Mr. Moyer has been busy all day; otherwise he would have called you himself." She turned and saw us standing there, and her eyes grew wide. "I understand your concerns, but I have to let you go now. We are quite busy. I will pass on the message to Mr. Moyer, as always."

Concern wrinkled itself into Eddie Moyer's brow, and I wondered what had happened to cause it. Who was Mr. Kratz, and why did the mention of his name bring such concern?

We said our good-byes, and I thanked the funeral director for his time. He nodded, smiled, then turned back toward his office. I'd learned a lot during the half hour I'd spent with Eddie Moyer, information I could use at a later date. Louise McGillicuddy's downcast expression caused several questions to run through my mind. She looked like a woman in distress, but why?

A strained smile tipped up the corners of her mouth. "Thank you for choosing Moyer's. I hope your visit was informative and will help you to make a decision." She ushered us to the door and opened it wide, as if to force us through.

I took a step outside into the sunlight. Sheila, however, lagged behind, finally turning to stare the woman down. "Hang on a minute, sister. We're not quite finished yet." I flashed her a warning look, but Sheila would not be shushed. "We're not just here to check out funeral policies."

I tried to squelch the groan, but it would not be squelched. Louise gripped the door handle, her eyes widening. Sheila forged ahead. "Sometimes it makes more sense not to beat around the bush, so let's just cut to the chase. We know that Fiona Kelly passed away here yesterday afternoon, and we'd like your help in figuring out who killed her."

Louise's face paled, and she ushered us onto the front walkway. "Who. . .killed her?" She spoke in a strained whisper. "Are you saying that she was murdered?" Her voice lowered until we could barely make out her words. "Are you sure?"

"We're not sure about anything," I offered, "but we were very good friends, and we are suspicious. We've put two and two together and come up with five."

"Look, don't you think we've had enough bad press?" Louise gave us a warning look then glanced around to make sure no one was listening in. "We're already worried about losing business, thanks to what happened. If you want to shut us down, then go right ahead and pursue this. But if you have half a heart, you'll leave and take your insinuations with you."

"Humph." Sheila crossed her arms at her chest. "How could anything hurt your business?"

"I'm pretty sure the DEAD BODY FOUND AT FUNERAL HOME headline in the local paper won't exactly cut into your business," I was quick to add. "So, if you could just tell us what happened yesterday afternoon. . .that would be a huge help. Then we'll be on our way."

A look of sadness washed over Louise's face. For a second, the forlorn look in her eyes almost made me feel sorry for her.

"Maggie Preston usually makes the deliveries for Fiona," Louise explained. "And I expected to see her yesterday with the casket spray for Mrs. Radisson. But Fiona came instead. Said Maggie had to go to Philly that afternoon. Those flowers were the last delivery Fiona Kelly ever made." Louise paused and dabbed her eyes. "Unless there are gardens in heaven."

I hadn't considered that possibility. If there were gardens in heaven, likely Fiona was digging in one right now.

"I've known Fiona for years, and I'm really going to miss her." Louise's downcast expression seemed genuine enough.

"Same here." I nodded. "That's why we're trying to figure out what happened."

"Where did she die, precisely?" Sheila reached for a pen.

"In Mr. Moyer's office."

Interesting. "And how long was she in there?" I queried.

"Quite awhile, actually. They were old friends, you know, but it had been awhile since her last visit, so they talked for some time. At least an hour. Maybe more."

She dove into a story about Fiona's ties to the Moyer family, but something off in the distance distracted me. I glanced across the parking lot to see the caretaker rising from his spot in the garden. The stiffness in his stance. . .the worry lines on his forehead. . .his concerned expression. . .I took note of all these things. Who was this fellow, and why did he give me reason to pause? If I didn't know any better, I'd have to say he'd been burying his troubles by digging in the dirt.

Louise continued with her story, finally ending with, "So we're all sad right now. We will miss Fiona terribly."

After a few more words, we wrapped up our conversation. I thanked Louise for her time, and then we took our first few steps toward the parking lot. As soon as we were out of hearing distance, Shelia turned to me with anger shooting from her eyes. "Let's get out of here, Annie. All of this funeral policy stuff just infuriates me."

"What? Why?"

"The whole prearranged funeral thing. Everything from *A* to *Z*. I can't afford to die. It's too expensive."

"Yeah, I know. But we have to be prepared, just in case. You heard what that Moyer fellow said. We don't want to leave the expenses for our loved ones to deal with. So that whole prepaid funeral thing does make sense."

"Still. . ." She shook her head, and a look of disgust registered on her face. "Their prices are exorbitant. Outrageous! And did you hear his excuse? Ooh, it makes me mad! Explain to me how a funeral home can raise its burial prices and blame it on the cost of living."

I couldn't help but chuckle, but just as quickly my laughter faded. I glanced through the open window into my car, horrified to find it. . .empty.

"Sheila." I turned to her with fear eking from

every pore. "Go around to the other side of the car and look into the backseat. Please tell me that the dogs are hiding. Or sleeping. Or something."

With her eyes widening, she shot to the far side of the car. One glance in the window was all it took. She looked back up at me and shook her head, whispering, "Annie, they're. . .they're gone."

5

I Need You. . .Like the Flowers Need the Rain

I call it the "white zone"—that place I slip into whenever I'm in a panic. My ears ring. I can't think clearly. Everything begins to spin. I see stars.

The minute we realized the dogs had disappeared, I slipped over into the white zone. Sure, I heard Sheila's voice. Saw her standing in front of me. But I couldn't have quoted anything she said. I vaguely remembered hearing her call out to the elderly caretaker, asking if he'd seen Sasha and Copper. Heard him mutter some sort of response. All of this I observed through a thick fog.

Somewhere along the way things started to come into focus again. I clutched the door handle in one hand and my purse in the other.

Sheila drew near and put her hand on my arm. "Annie, it's going to be okay. We'll drive through the cemetery and look for them. I'm sure they're still here."

"W–what if they're not?" I felt the sting of tears in my eyes but pushed them away. As much as I complained about my puppies, I could never live without them. And to think that they might be running rampant through a cemetery, of all places, left me feeling sick inside.

Sheila gave me a confident look. "Let's not panic yet."

Easy for her to say.

"I'll do the driving. You take the passenger seat." Sheila grabbed my purse and fumbled around until she came up with the keys. She climbed in, and I somehow managed to follow suit. Minutes later we drove from one section of the large cemetery to another in search of two fast-on-their-feet dachshunds.

I'd almost given up when Sheila's voice rang out. "Annie, look!" She hit the brakes, and we came to a squealing stop as she pointed to a row of headstones on our right. I breathed a sigh of relief as I saw Copper leaning against the largest one, panting.

Catching my breath, I reached for the door handle. Getting out of the car without startling him might be a bit tricky. He had a tendency to run when called, so I needed to handle myself carefully. If only I had something to offer him as a treat. Anything.

Easing my way out the door, I placed my feet on the ground and tiptoed toward him. I'd almost reached the little monster when the caretaker pulled up in a golf cart, making far too much racket. Copper looked our way and took off running. I sprinted after him like a high school track star in the making, but a voice from behind brought me to a grinding halt.

"Don't worry, ma'am," the caretaker shouted as the golf cart whizzed past me. "I'll get him."

I watched with relief as he drew near Copper, who had finally slowed his pace. Something in the old man's face must've won the little mongrel over, because he came when called—Copper, not the caretaker.

Trying to overcome my emotions, I made my way toward them. "I can't thank you enough." Taking the pup into my arms, I both scolded and praised him, all at the same time.

Seeing the older fellow up close put a whole new spin on things. His soft blue eyes reminded me of my father's. The thin wisps of white hair put me in mind of my grandfather, and a sad reminiscent feeling came over me at once, especially when I noticed the fellow's farming overalls. Yep. My grandfather, through and through.

He pulled off a glove and extended a wrinkled, leathery hand my way. "Jim Roever." After a bit of a smirk, he added, "They call me the Grim Reaper."

Roever. Reaper. I got it. Clever, for a fellow who tended the grounds in a graveyard.

"Annie Peterson." I shifted Copper to my shoulder and shook the man's hand with vigor. "Again, I can't thank you enough."

"Well, I'm pretty good with animals."

I snapped to attention and began to search among the headstones, realizing that we weren't quite finished yet. Turning to Mr. Roever, I asked if he'd seen Sasha. "She's a little smaller than Copper and a lighter shade of red."

"Noticed 'em both when they were in the car," he said. "They were yapping to beat the band."

"Yikes. I'm sorry about that." I craned my neck, trying to locate Sasha. Where, oh where, was my baby?

"Well, they wanted out, that much was certain. But I didn't figure they could squeeze through such a small opening." He offered up a shrug. "Guess I should've kept a better eye on them."

"Dachshunds can flatten like pancakes," I explained,

my gaze still darting from place to place. "I should've thought about that before leaving them in the car. This is my own fault."

"No, it–it's mine." Sheila appeared behind me. "If I hadn't been so impatient, you would have taken them home like you wanted." She shook her head, and I noticed that her eyes glistened. "Will you forgive me?"

"Nothing to forgive."

With Jim Roever's help, we spent the next half hour in a frantic search for Sasha. At a quarter to twelve, knowing that Sheila would be late for her lunch date with her husband, we finally gave up. Forcing my words past the lump in my throat, I gave Mr. Roever my phone number and committed to return the next day with flyers in hand. Oh how I wished I could return this afternoon, but my backlog of work wouldn't allow it. My heart broke, just thinking about Sasha roaming around lost.

"I'll keep an eye out for her," he promised. "I'm sure she'll turn up before long, and I'll call you right away when she does." He gave me a reassuring look. "I've worked at this cemetery for thirty-five years, and I know every square inch of this property. If she's here, I'll find her."

"Thank you so much." I wanted to give the man a hug but decided against it.

Sheila took the wheel once more, and I sat in the passenger seat with Copper in my lap as we pulled away. I didn't even try to stop the tears or the memories that flooded over me as we made our way down the winding roads toward Clarksborough.

I thought of the many times Sasha and I had cuddled together on the couch. How she'd slept at my feet every night for the past three years. How she'd acclimated to having a new dog in the house a few short months ago. I remembered the time she'd OD'd on chocolate and we'd almost lost her. Most of all, I thought of the faithful companion she'd been to me over the years, even helping out with my crime-solving adventures. Had we really been through all that just to lose her now?

Sheila reached into her purse for a tissue and passed it my way. "It's okay to cry, Annie. I know Sasha means the world to you."

I hated to admit how much. With both my girls flying the coop and Devin about to graduate from high school, the dogs had filled a void in my life. It wasn't something I talked about—much, anyway—but I genuinely loved my disobedient duo, mischievous or not. Only, now the duo was a solo. I gazed into Copper's sad brown eyes. How would we manage without Sasha in the mix?

Forcing my negative thoughts aside, I reached into my purse and pulled out my phone. "I'd better get this over with."

Warren answered on the second ring. "Hi there, beautiful. I just picked up the phone to call you."

"O—oh?"

"I'm headed to lunch. Want to meet me at the diner? It's grilled chicken Caesar salad day. I know that's your favorite."

"Yes, well. . ." I swallowed hard and pushed the words out. "Warren, I have something to tell you."

The tears started in force now, and I barely managed to relay the story. When I finished, Warren hesitated a moment before responding.

"Annie, what in the world were you doing at a cemetery?"

Hmm. I hadn't lied to him about going—simply omitted it from our earlier conversations. Besides, he knew me better than anyone. Surely he knew. . .

"You're thinking Fiona was murdered, aren't you?" Before I could answer, he jumped back in. "Candy talked to me last night after church. She was afraid of this. I told her it would pass. After all, there's no reason to suspect foul play."

"Well, I—"

"Annie, don't you think you're jumping the gun this time?"

An elongated pause gave me the time I needed to work up the necessary courage to answer. "I'm not the only one. Sheila is—"

"Sheila is with you?"

"Mm-hmm." Had I left out that part, too?

"Orin was at the bank a few minutes ago. Said he and Sheila were having lunch at the diner at noon. Asked if we wanted to meet them. Does he know she's there?"

"I, um. . ." After a sigh, I added, "I doubt it."

"I see. So the two of you are in cahoots."

Hmm. I guess you could put it that way. Only our cahooting didn't really get us anywhere.

"I'll drop off Copper at the house, and then Sheila and I will join you for lunch," I assured him. "And I'm sorry I didn't tell you about going to the funeral home.

But I had a great talk with the director. He gave me a ton of information about planning ahead for your funeral."

"Planning ahead for *my* funeral?" Warren sounded confused.

"Well, your funeral. My funeral. Our funerals. You know what I mean."

"What has you thinking about all of this, Annie? What's with this sudden fixation on death? Is it because of Fiona, or is there something else going on?"

I didn't want to tell him that I'd spent a more-than-average amount of time over the past few months thinking about Judy Blevins's premature death. Didn't want to remind him that she had passed away in her early fifties and that I would cross over to fifty in less than a year. Didn't want him to know that I'd secretly struggled with hidden fears regarding my premenopausal body.

Someday, but not today.

As we started to say our good-byes, Warren interrupted me. "Annie?"

"Yes?"

"You. . .you looked everywhere for Sasha?"

Was that a catch I heard in his voice?

"We did."

"And Copper's okay? You're sure?"

I wrapped the pup in my arms as I whispered, "Mm-hmm."

"Well, take him home and then come to the diner. I'll fill Orin in. Oh, and Annie. . ."

"Yes?"

"Just so you know. . .I plan to grow old with you.

To drive you crazy after I retire. To putter around in the yard and plant a vegetable garden. To buy an RV and travel. Together. So don't get any ideas about heading off to the hereafter just yet. I need you, honey."

My eyes filled once again. "Even if I'm as nutty as a fruitcake?"

"I happen to be one of the few people on planet Earth who actually likes fruitcake," he responded. "So don't change a thing."

We ended the call with the same "I love you" as always, but the words seemed to carry a greater depth this time. Lord willing, we *would* grow old together.

In the meantime, one missing dachshund would very likely age me. . .overnight.

6

My Wild Irish Rose

We spent the better part of the next two days hanging "Missing" posters all over Clark County, focusing on the town of Wallop. Surely someone had taken Sasha in by now and would call us. Maybe the $500 reward would serve as a motivation. Warren had been gracious enough to suggest it and hadn't even flinched at the amount.

I pushed back the lump in my throat as I hung the posters. Looking at the photo of Sasha—her big brown eyes, long pointed nose, squatty little legs, beautiful red coat—made me miss her more than ever. Would I ever see my devilish doxie again?

I knew I should jump back into the wedding plans. There were so many details left undone, and Candy needed me. I needed to shift back into mother-of-the-bride gear. And now that the W.O.W. group was taking on the gardening project with my daughter's reception in mind, I really ought to offer to help out. And take care of my clients. And do some laundry. And make sure my husband and son had a hot meal on the table occasionally.

Still, I could hardly think straight with my baby gone. Nothing felt the same around the Peterson household without Sasha. Copper moped while inside and spent his time in the backyard searching under ever bush, every rock. He didn't even bother to enter into his usual yap-fest with the Maltese. He suffered from depression, no doubt. I know I did. Even Warren behaved strangely. He didn't bother to scold Copper after an incident that involved his tennis shoes. Very telling.

On Saturday morning, many of Clarksborough's residents gathered together at the church to pay tribute to Fiona Kelly one last time. I'd secretly been dreading the funeral service but never more so than when we pulled into the parking lot and saw the hearse with the word MOYER'S written on the side. Something about all of this, especially in combination with Sasha's disappearance, affected me deeply. Was it because Fiona wasn't much older than me when she passed away? Like Judy Blevins? Like that woman in the casket at the funeral home. . .Mrs. Radisson?

Maybe Warren was right. I *was* fixating. And I needed to stop. Likely I had many good years ahead of me. And even if I didn't. . .

I refused to think about that possibility. I had another daughter to marry off. I had a son who would graduate the day after the wedding. I had grandchildren to one day usher into the world. I had a husband who needed and loved me. And work to do. My days—long or short—were in the Lord's hands, no one else's. Why not just enjoy the time I had left?

Warren interrupted my ponderings by gently placing his hand on my back. "You ready, hon?"

I looked over at him and nodded. *As ready as I'll ever be.*

We worked our way through the crowd, and I paused to give Sheila a hug as we entered the building.

"You okay?" I asked.

She nodded then gripped my hand. "On a scale of one to ten, I'm about a three." She glanced down at her snazzy black dress and added, " 'Course, if you factor in the new dress, that might push it up to a four."

Warren and I made our way into the sanctuary and slipped into a pew about two-thirds of the way back. I knew Devin couldn't attend, what with school and all, but I half expected to see the girls. Ah yes. They were up at the front, offering their condolences to Fiona's family. I winced as I focused on the family section. Diedre and her husband, Patrick, sat in the front pew, along with a couple of Fiona's siblings. Other than that, the area looked rather vacant.

Thankfully, the sanctuary did not. What Fiona lacked in family, she made up for in friends. I pondered that a moment. She'd made such an impact on our little community. People loved her so much—as evidenced by the crowd. I couldn't help but wonder who might show up for my "big day," as Eddie Moyer had called it. Had I impacted lives? Would people turn out to wave their good-byes? To shed tears because losing me had created a hole in their lives? I hoped so.

Though I'd done my best to avoid looking at the casket, I finally decided to get it over with. Thanks to my chat with Eddie Moyer the other day, I now knew the various levels of pricing. Fiona's casket was a lower-end 20-gauge steel model with protective Monoguard. . . the Econoline design, to be precise. Still, it was lovely—sort of a silvery gray with a white crepe lining. And the large spray of coral-colored roses on top seemed to suit the occasion. Diedre had always called Fiona their "wild

Irish rose," a name the beloved florist had loved.

As the clock struck ten, the girls joined us. I noticed Maggie Preston slip in. I'd known her for years, of course—through Fiona. A bubbly woman in her midthirties, Maggie had moved to Clarksborough after going through a difficult divorce. She and Fiona had that in common. Well, that and their love for flowers. They'd worked side by side, turning Flowers by Fiona into quite the rage in Clark County.

Maggie nodded as she passed by then headed to the front and took her seat with Diedre and Patrick in the family section, right where she belonged. As I gazed at her tearstained face, my prior suspicions melted away. Surely someone who loved Fiona this much never could have murdered her. Right? If, in fact, she'd been murdered at all. I still had to wonder if my speculations were ill-founded.

My gaze shifted as the pallbearers entered and took their seats. Garrett looked somewhat forlorn, as did his older brother, Sean, a prematurely balding thirtysomething. The two Caine brothers were as different in temperament as could possibly be. Garrett lived up to the Irish meaning of his name: "brave spearman." Candy found humor in that on occasion, but I thought he was warrior material. I'd never met anyone as fearless. Not that a computer tech necessarily needed to be fearless. Sean, who was working on his master's in Renaissance Literature, ran a little more on the bookworm side. I could almost see him now, digging in the garden with his mother and quoting Shakespeare. A sensitive soul.

I took note of Eddie Moyer standing near the

front, saying a few hushed words to Pastor Miller. Afterward, as the overhead music lowered, our pastor approached the podium, ready to begin the service. A stirring at the back of the auditorium distracted me. I turned back to see that Sergeant O'Henry had entered the room. Sergeant O'Henry? Sure, he attended the church, but to come in uniform? Did he have other reasons for being here? Were we all being watched, perhaps?

I tried not to think of that as the service began. Tried not to dwell on it afterward as we caravanned to Wallop for the burial. But when O'Henry followed us back to the church for the family luncheon—which I'd agreed to help with—my suspicions mounted.

From the church's kitchen, I kept a watchful eye on the good sergeant. He made his way from person to person, pausing at length as he visited with Maggie Preston.

Yes, something was surely afoot. And it would only be a matter of time before I figured it out.

"A penny for your thoughts."

I turned as I heard Janetta Mullins's voice. "Oh, I, um. . ."

"Having a hard day?" Her brow winkled in concern.

"Yeah." I hated to admit it, but I was.

"I heard about Sasha." She gave me a sympathetic look, and my heart lurched. "I want you to know how sorry I am and that I'm praying."

"Thanks." I sighed, contemplating the fact that my dog had landed at the top of the church's prayer list. "I feel a little silly worrying about a dog when we're at a funeral for a good friend. Losing Judy and Fiona so close together has been such a wake-up call, especially with both of them dying so young."

"I know what you mean." Janetta turned her attention to getting the food ready, but I could tell her thoughts were elsewhere. "I've had the oddest thoughts go through my mind over the past few days. It's almost. . ."

"Morbid?"

She turned to me with a look of relief on her face. "Yes, how did you know?"

"Been there, done that. I'm wondering if we're all just menopausal."

"Well, that, too." A whimsical smile lit her face but quickly faded. "I've been a little hyperfocused on my own death."

"Me, too," I admitted. "Seems like all the women in our age group are. . ."

"Dying?"

No sooner had the words slipped out of my mouth than a revelation struck. *That's* why I'd been so intent on proving that Fiona did not die of natural causes. I didn't *want* her death to be natural. If she passed away because of a physical ailment, especially something undetected, that meant we were all open to the same possibility. But if I could prove that someone had done her in. . .

Good grief. Now I'm wishing for a murder to avoid thinking about my own mortality.

A noise behind us alerted me to the fact that someone had joined us. I looked over at Evelyn, who flashed a warm smile. "Janetta. Annie. Thank you both so much for helping out with the meal. I know the family members are grateful."

"No problem."

"And Annie"—she took me by the hand—"I heard about Sasha. I've been praying. I just know she's going to turn up. She's got to."

"Thank you. You're probably the fifth or sixth person to tell me that. My phone's been ringing off the wall." *Goodness. I hope the grieving family is getting as many condolences as I am.*

Janetta turned the conversation in a different direction, likely as an attempt to lift our spirits. "I want you to know how excited I am about the Bible study." Her eyes lit up as she spoke. "I've been reading the thirty-first chapter of Proverbs, trying to get geared up. And I have a list of vegetable dishes to serve as snacks."

"Wonderful." Evelyn clasped her hands together then turned to me. "What about you, Annie? Are you getting excited?"

About digging in the dirt? Tilling the soil?

"Tickled pink." I did my best to act enthused. Perhaps by Wednesday afternoon I would be.

Evelyn spent the next several minutes talking with us about her plans for the courtyard, but my thoughts shifted to Maggie Preston. Something in her countenance had changed when O'Henry spoke to her. I saw the worry lines. Read the concern in her eyes.

As the luncheon drew to a close, I made my way over to visit with her. I'd been meaning to do so all day but just hadn't found the right opportunity. Now with Sergeant O'Henry gone, perhaps I could broach the subject of Fiona's untimely death without raising too many suspicions.

Maggie greeted me with a smile. She reached out

and took my hand. "Annie, I'm so glad you're here. Fiona loved you so much."

"And I loved her, too." After a brief pause, I added, "It's hard to believe she's gone. She was so healthy, so vivacious."

"The most health-conscious woman I've ever known," Maggie agreed then paused with a hint of a smile, the first I'd seen from her all day. "Didn't you think the roses were beautiful?"

"Perfect."

"My wild Irish rose." We spoke the words in unison.

I paused a moment then asked a question that had been on my mind for a while. "Maggie, do you plan to keep the shop open?"

"Yes." Her smile broadened. "Fiona left the shop to me in her will, and I'm committed to keeping it going."

Aha.

"Won't change the name, either. Everything will stay just as it is, at least for now."

"Good girl." After a few seconds to absorb everything she'd said, I asked if I could come by the shop on Monday morning to fill her in on Candy's wedding plans, and she agreed.

Maggie's eyes exuded weariness. I placed my hand on her arm. "I'm going to be praying for you. This is a lot to handle."

"It's been so hard." She lowered her voice and looked around, as if worried about being overheard. "And it's getting harder as the minutes tick by. Did you see Sergeant O'Henry?" When I nodded, she added. "He got me so worked up."

"Oh?"

"He questioned me like I was a suspect or something. Can you believe that?"

I knew it!

Maggie's eyes filled with tears. "I loved Fiona like a mother. She was nothing but good to me."

"What did he say?"

"Just asked where I was on the day she died, that sort of thing. Asked why she'd made the run to Moyer's instead of me." Maggie shook her head. "I had an appointment that afternoon. "I've been. . ." Her voice trailed off. "Anyway, I was in Philly, and Fiona was doing me a favor. Nothing new there."

"She loved you very much."

Maggie nodded. "There was never any doubt in my mind. But now that O'Henry has got me all riled up, I can't help but wonder. . .two things, actually."

"What?"

"First. . ." She gave me a thoughtful look. "If Fiona had never gone to the funeral home that day, would she still be alive? And second, if I'd gone as planned, would *I* still be alive?"

Maggie's words rocked me to the core. It had never occurred to me that someone other than Fiona might've been the intended victim.

Had I, perhaps, overlooked a major piece to the puzzle?

7

TIPTOE THROUGH THE TULIPS

Sheila always says, "If you can't see the bright side of life, polish the dull side." That's exactly what I set out to do early Monday morning as I made my way to the flower shop to meet with Maggie.

My heart still ached whenever I thought of Sasha, but I had to forge ahead. Several questions flitted through my mind as I steered my way to the center of town. First, had Fiona really been murdered, or had I jumped the gun to somehow put my own mind at ease? Second, if my suspicions were right, had she been the intended target, or had she, as Maggie suggested, simply been in the wrong place at the wrong time? Her death at the funeral home raised far too many questions in my mind. After all, who died that close to a cemetery? Other than, say, a funeral director or one of the other employees?

A shiver ran down my spine as I remembered my earlier conversation with Eddie Moyer. If only I'd known at the time that Fiona had passed away in that very room! How calm and unassuming he'd appeared as he discussed funeral policies. How suave. How businesslike. Did he harbor secrets? Should I, like Copper, look under every bush, every rock, until I figured out what made Eddie Moyer tick?

And what about Louise? Something about the woman left me feeling unsettled. Either she was the nervous type or she was up to something. Sure, she didn't look like the sort to commit a murder, but who did?

I arrived at the flower shop at exactly nine o'clock, just as Maggie opened up for the day. As I sat in the parking lot and gazed at the FLOWERS BY FIONA sign, my heart twisted. I didn't want to go inside. How could I face the flower shop without its kindhearted owner?

Without pausing to overthink the situation, I made my way to the door. The bell above jangled as I entered. The heavenly scent swept me away, as always. Flowers in every color, shape, and size exuded an intoxicating aroma. I stopped short, drawing in a deep breath. The combination of all those fragrances almost caused me to swoon.

Determined to stay focused, I made my way to the counter in the hopes of finding Maggie. I called out her name, and she came out of the back room. She took one look at me, and her face lit into a smile. "Annie." I noticed the weariness in her eyes as she spoke. "I'm so glad you're here. It's good to see you again."

"You, too." I gave her a hug, and we got to work, updating her on Candy's order. Several times the bell above the door interrupted us. During those times, Maggie rose to wait on other customers. I didn't mind. In fact, I was happy to see the shop still doing such great business. Many of the visitors were just that, folks stopping in to share their stories about Fiona and talk about what a great friend she'd been.

"I couldn't decide what to bring to offer my condolences," one older woman admitted. "Seemed a little silly to bring flowers to a florist."

Maggie got a kick out of that one and told the woman she'd brought the best gift of all—herself.

On and on the customers came, in a steady stream. Maggie seemed a bit out of sorts—who could blame her?—but she still managed to stay on top of her orders. I watched in amazement as she worked. Her flower-arranging skills were nothing to thumb your nose at. She seemed to be the perfect candidate to pick up where Fiona left off.

Still, I noticed how her hands trembled on occasion. Picked up on the anxiety in her face. Paid close attention to how pale she'd been the last few times I'd seen her. How she wouldn't look folks in the eye.

Very suspicious.

Or not. Maybe she was just feeling the strain of losing her dearest friend.

After the crowd thinned, Maggie and I turned our attention to Candy's wedding order once again. I wanted to go over everything since Maggie had been in Philly during our last meeting. She found the paperwork and studied it intently, finally looking up at me with a confident smile.

"I'll order the daisies, making sure they come in a couple of days before the wedding. Then I'll get the bouquets and boutonnieres made. And I'll put together the prettiest arrangements for the sanctuary you ever saw. And what if we work on the centerpieces for the tables together?"

"Of course. Sounds like fun."

"I've been thinking about using these cute little watering cans to hold the flowers." She held one up to show me. "What do you think? I mentioned it to

Candy, and she seemed to take to the idea."

"Sounds perfect." I chuckled. "Did she tell you that she's been dreaming of a daisy-filled wedding since she was a little girl?"

"No. Why daisies?"

"I think it's that whole 'He loves me, he loves me not' thing," I explained. "She was always the sort to get her heart broken by boys, even as a preteen. She always fell in love so easily, though that love wasn't always returned."

"Aw, that's sad." The edges of Maggie's lips turned down in a pout.

"I know. So imagine how happy she was to finally meet Garrett, after so many disappointments. She said she wants to fill the whole place with daisies as a reminder that he loves her. And vice versa."

"Fabulous idea, and one of the sweetest stories I've ever heard." Maggie's eyes filled with tears. "I only wish Fiona could've been here to enjoy it."

"Oh, trust me, Candy told her." I felt the edges of my lips shift upward as I shared the rest of the story. "Fiona told Candy she'd plucked more than her share of petals over the years, too."

"Yeah, I know Fiona's story well. She faced quite a few struggles in the love department." Maggie released a long sigh. "We had a lot in common that way."

After taking note of the look of pain in her eyes, I did my best to shift the conversation. We talked for quite some time about my daughter's big day. Then around ten o'clock, after waiting on a couple more customers, Maggie offered to brew some tea.

"I know how you like it." She winked. "Earl Grey. . ."

"Heavy on the cream." We spoke in unison.

Yep, she knew me pretty well. Interesting, in light of the fact that the woman had never brewed me a cup of tea in her life. Still, Fiona had. And Maggie must've been paying attention. I looked at her with an investigator's eye, deep in thought. If Maggie Preston ever decided to give up on floral work, she might just make it as a supersleuth.

She returned minutes later with two cups of steaming tea. Janetta Mullins entered the shop at the same time with a platter of sweets in hand. Talk about a happy coincidence.

"These were left over from the get-together on Saturday," she explained as she drew near. "I thought maybe you'd want to share them with your customers."

Maggie thanked her then went to the back to fetch another cup of tea and returned to join us. As she took her seat, she reached to grab a chocolate croissant. "Fiona would slap this out of my hand. She was also so good about limiting her sweets. And mine."

"As long as you're not diabetic, I don't see how an occasional treat can hurt." Janetta pursed her lips. "Sometimes we just need a little spoonful of sugar to help the medicine go down. Or, in this case, to help us swallow the sadness."

The minute I heard the word "sugar," I thought of my dimpled thighs. Forcing the image to the back of my mind, I reached for a cookie.

"Mmm." I talked between bites. "You're the best, Janetta. I can't wait to see what you come up with for Candy's wedding."

"Oh, I have so many great ideas in mind." She slipped into caterer extraordinaire gear, and I had to smile. I hadn't known Janetta well until the past year or so, but she felt like a sister to me now. A kindred spirit.

"So, tell me. . ." Janetta turned to Maggie. "What's going to happen to the shop? You'll need help, right?"

"I'll be hiring someone soon to help out around here," Maggie explained. "But I think I can manage till then."

An idea came to mind right away. "My son, Devin, is looking for a job. Maybe he'd be interested." No sooner were the words out then I slapped a hand over my mouth. Sure, my football-playing, testosterone-driven son had been looking for a part-time job, but in a flower shop? He'd likely have my head for suggesting such a thing.

"I'd love to talk with him." Maggie smiled. "He'd be a lot of fun to train."

"Um, sure." I'd been training him for eighteen years, and it hadn't all been fun.

Janetta took charge of the conversation at that point, pointing out that the teens in the community would surely flock to the shop if my handsome son worked inside. I wasn't so sure. In spite of his winning smile and his strategic moves on the field, Devin hadn't exactly won over the girls, at least not yet. He felt it had something to do with his "packaging," as he called it. Okay, so he was a little on the chubby side. What great football player wasn't? Surely the right girl would come along at just the right time. In the meantime, he might just make a fine florist.

After a few more minutes of conversation, Janetta looked at her watch and gasped. "I've got to get out of here. I have to bake a cake for a birthday party and put together the menu for the W.O.W. group Wednesday night." She looked my way. "You'll be there, won't you, Annie?"

"I'll be there." With bells on.

As soon as Janetta left, I turned my attention to Maggie. I'd been working up the courage to broach a sensitive subject.

"I, um, I've been thinking about what you said the other day after the funeral."

"Oh?" Maggie's brow wrinkled as she turned my way. "Which part?"

"The part where you insinuated that Fiona might not have been the intended target."

"Ah." Her brow wrinkled as she spoke. "I don't know why I said that. It just slipped out. I don't want you to think I. . ."

I leaned in a bit closer and lowered my voice, just in case anyone entered the store. "Don't apologize. I think you might've been on to something. Maybe the murderer, if there was a murderer, really *was* after someone else." I reached for another of Janetta's wonderful cookies and took a bite. "And I'm suspicious about something else. Did you know that Fiona died in Eddie Moyer's office?"

"Sure." Maggie nodded. "But it doesn't surprise me that she was in his office. They'd known each other for years, like I told the sergeant. And I know she'd been worried about Eddie. Maybe she had finally worked up the courage to talk to him."

"About?"

"Well, she had some concerns. I think she wanted

to visit with him. . .to get a few things off her chest."
Maggie shrugged. "Trust me, I have enough going
on in my own life right now. I don't need to borrow
trouble from anyone else. In other words, I wouldn't
feel comfortable sharing the details, at least not yet."

"I see."

The phone rang and Maggie took the call. As she
took an order by phone, I thought about her words.
Did someone have it in for Eddie Moyer, perhaps?
Had he been the intended murder victim? Or was he
involved in something underhanded?

After Maggie ended her call, I shared my thoughts.
"I've had a brilliant beyond brilliant idea."

"Oh?"

"I wonder if you would mind letting me look
through your receipts from the past four or five
months."

"Um, okay." Maggie went behind the counter and
pulled open a drawer. "What am I looking for?"

"The name of anyone who ordered a casket spray
for a family member." After a brief pause, I added,
"Just make sure it was delivered to Moyer's, not one of
the other funeral homes."

"Goodness. There were dozens of deaths in the
past month alone. Do you have any idea how many
people pass away in Clark County in a month's time?"

"I'm just playing a hunch here, but I have a
suspicion that there might be more than one person
unhappy with a funeral director."

She looked stunned. "So you're planning to contact
every person who used Moyer's services to bury a loved
one, to see if, perchance, they wanted to murder Eddie?"

I swallowed the last of my cookie before answering. "I know, I know. Sounds far-fetched. But what's the harm?" Brushing my hands on my jeans, I gave her a sheepish smile.

She gave me one of those "What are you up to, Annie Peterson?" looks. I knew it well. Had seen it on my husband's face a couple hundred times. After a moment, she shrugged and gave her response: "I guess it wouldn't hurt to look."

With her permission, I thumbed through the stack of receipts, writing down the names and phone numbers of folks who had lost a loved one. Near the very bottom of the pile, I stumbled across a receipt with a name that stopped me cold. *Roger Kratz.*

"Kratz. Kratz."

I gripped the paper, and a memory flooded over me. Louise McGillicuddy's phone call, the one that had put such a look of concern on Eddie Moyer's face. *"Mr. Kratz, we've been over this several times. . . . I understand your concerns, but I have to let you go. . . ."*

I looked over the receipt once more. Was *this* Mr. Kratz *that* Mr. Kratz? If so, what could he tell me about the death of Fiona Kelly?

I'd never know if I sat here all day. Determined to play this hunch, I headed for the door.

8

FLOWER IN THE RAIN

As I pulled out of the flower shop parking lot, I took note of the ominous skies above. Hopefully it wouldn't rain just yet. I had a crime to investigate, and cloudy skies could lead to a cloudy outcome. I headed off to Wallop to locate Mr. Kratz's house but found myself thinking about Sasha every step of the way.

Passing the cemetery, I felt the familiar lump rise up in my throat. *Sasha! My sweet baby! Where are you?* Perhaps, if time allowed, I could swing by Moyer's on my way home. What would it hurt to take another look around? To do a little searching? To speak to Jim Roever? Maybe he'd located my little darling but hadn't had time to call.

Glancing at the slip of paper on the passenger seat, I focused on Roger Kratz's address: 123 BUTTERCUP. After a bit of searching, I pulled up in front of his house and put the car into park. With a full heart, I thought about the man inside who'd so recently lost his wife. I wondered how old she was at the time of her passing. How she'd died. How he was coping.

I also wondered how he would feel about a total stranger dropping in on him. Or how my husband would take the news that I'd gone into a strange man's house alone when he thought I was at home editing manuscripts. I shifted the car back into drive and kept driving. Maybe I'd be better served by calling Mr. Kratz first. And Warren, of course.

Pulling the car into the parking lot of a small coffee shop, I reached for the phone and punched in the number for Mr. Kratz. He answered on the fourth ring with an abrupt, "Hello?"

"Could I speak with Roger Kratz, please?"

"You've got him."

He had that irritated sound to his voice, the same sound I'd often heard Warren use with salespeople. Maybe I'd better just cut to the chase, put this guy's mind at ease.

"Mr. Kratz, my name is Annie Peterson. I live in Clarksborough. First, let me offer my condolences on the loss of your wife."

"What are you selling?"

"Oh, I'm not—"

"I'm not interested in a new headstone, and I don't want to name a star after her. I've already bankrupted myself to pay for her funeral, so don't start up with your sob stories about how much better I'll feel if I just donate money to your charity in her honor. You can forget it."

His words threw me. "I, um, I'm not calling about any of those things. Actually, I've been visiting with the fine folks at Moyer's funeral home and am thinking about purchasing a prepaid funeral policy. I thought maybe you'd chat with me about your experience with them."

"Who told you to make this call?"

"Oh, no one. I—"

"Was it that McGillicuddy woman? Did she give you my number? If so, I'll. . ." He began to spew his thoughts about Louise and Eddie, explaining how they would pay for giving out private information. For the first time, I realized that my investigative work might be putting Moyer's employees in harm's way.

"No, sir." I stopped him before he could say much more. "Louise didn't give me your information. Neither did Mr. Moyer. I tracked down several names and numbers of folks in the area who've done business with the funeral home, so please don't think they're up to something. They don't even know we're speaking."

"So what'd you do? Hunt me down though the obituaries? I've heard about you folks. You watch the obits to see when families are burying their loved ones; then you rob their homes."

"No sir. I've never robbed anyone in my life. Nor do I plan to."

"Then you're a sure sight better than that Eddie Moyer."

Okay. Now we were talking. "W—what do you mean?"

"I mean, he's into highway robbery. Masquerades as a funeral service. Some service. Sure, he puts on the nice suit, the happy face. But all the while he's robbing you blind."

"Mr. Kratz, I know you don't know me from Adam. But I'm in Wallop, sitting in front of the PA Perk. Would you be willing to meet me for a cup of coffee? My treat. I'd love to talk with you about your experience with Moyer's."

I heard him inhale a breath. "Will it keep you from buying the funeral policy?"

"Maybe."

"Then I'll come. But you'd better be prepared for an earful. And I hope you've got a wad of money. The Perk has great cinnamon-swirl coffee cake."

"You've got it."

After ending the call, I had just enough time to telephone Warren and let him know my plans. He didn't seem surprised to hear that I'd decided to spend my afternoon on the case. In fact, he sounded strangely calm. "Just be careful, Annie. Stay in a public place and keep your cell phone with you at all times."

"Will do."

I entered the coffee shop seconds later, pausing for a moment to drink in the delicious aroma that enveloped me. "Mmm." I might be a tea lover, but there was something about the smell of brewed coffee that made my head swim—in a good way. And what visual delights greeted me! I made my way through the shop, staring at bags of specialty coffees, expensive grinders, and high-end espresso machines. Wow. PA Perk was really picking up steam. Pun intended.

Taking a seat at a table near the door, I pulled out my sleuthing notebook and a pen. Less than five minutes later, the bell above the door alerted me to the fact that someone had arrived. I looked up and saw an older man easing his way inside. His slightly stooped appearance gave me a clear view of his thinning silver hair—what little he had left, anyway.

I found myself distracted by something else, though. Knobby knees poked out beneath his khaki-colored shorts. His worn black belt held up the pants. Almost. I allowed my gaze to travel up to the threadbare button-up shirt with its faded blue stripes—minus a couple of buttons—which he wore over a dingy white T-shirt. His wire-rimmed spectacles appeared to be slightly smudged. Perhaps the thing that stood out most, however, even more than the black crew socks, was the sour look on his face. Clearly this fellow trusted no one, especially not a nosy female.

I offered my most relaxed and gracious smile as I extended my hand. "Mr Kratz?"

He grunted as he eased his way down into a chair opposite me. "I'll take my coffee black. None of that fancy foamy stuff on top. And cinnamon-swirl—"

"Coffee cake." I gave up on the handshake idea and joined him as he finished the sentence. "You've got it."

Making my way through the crowded tables, I settled into line. All the while, I contemplated my options. How much should I tell this guy?

With the line so long, I had a few minutes to pray about it. I finally reached the register and placed our order. Afterward, the kid behind the counter—the one with the BARISTA tag—caught my attention with a raised brow.

"You with that old guy?" he whispered.

"Well, yes. . ." I turned back to look at Roger, who pulled a receipt from his pocket and gazed at it intently. "Sort of."

"He's been in here before." The barista spoke in a low voice. "Pitched a fit over our prices. He's a tightwad."

"Well, I'm paying today." I winked at the kid, hoping he'd take the hint and stop talking so loudly. No point in scaring off my suspect, after all. If, in fact, Roger Kratz was a suspect. I hadn't quite decided yet.

Minutes later I returned to the table with two steaming cups of coffee and a couple of pieces of cake. I set them down with a forced smile.

"Let's not beat around the bush." Roger's eyes narrowed into slits. "You want to hear about Moyer's. I've got plenty to share."

I decided not to interrupt him. Probably a good thing, since he seemed to have a lot on his mind.

"My wife, Betty, passed away four months ago. We were married for forty-three years."

"I–I'm so sorry."

He shrugged, and I watched in rapt silence as his eyes misted over. "She battled emphysema for the last fifteen years of her life. Terrible situation. She was in so much pain toward the end and there was nothing I could do to help her. When she died. . ." He drew in a deep breath then continued, "I went to Moyer's, of course. Everyone in Wallop does. They're supposed to be the best in the county and the most reasonable."

"I'm not sure about the most reasonable part," I threw in. "None of his funeral plans sounded terribly economical to me."

"Well, these folks in the funeral industry get you with the big stuff up front then nickel and dime you to death on the tail end. And it all adds up quick."

"I must admit, the prices took me by surprise. I had no idea you could spend over twenty-five-thousand dollars on a funeral."

Kratz nodded his head. "Yes, and if you go with a lesser plan, Moyer makes you feel like you're not doing right by your loved one. That was the most offensive thing of all."

As Kratz continued to share, I remembered something Eddie Moyer had said that day in his office: *"I've been in this business for years and can tell you, grieving friends and family members are hardly in the right state of mind to be making tough choices."*

I'd never considered the fact that Moyer might actually be taking advantage of that.

"Betty had life insurance," Roger explained, "but even at that, you have to pay with cash, check, or credit card up front—and none of those options worked for me. Folks in my position have to take out a loan until the insurance pays. That can take months, depending on whether an autopsy is done and how long it takes to get the results."

"Whoa. I had no idea." That prepaid plan was looking better every day. I'd always assumed that my life insurance would cover all the costs of the funeral. Never considered that my loved ones might have to actually borrow money to lay me to rest. That didn't exactly make me feel like resting.

Mr. Kratz kept talking, oblivious to my internal ponderings. "Yes. So, a twelve-thousand-dollar funeral at 21 percent interest was what we settled on."

"Yikes."

"By the time all was said and done, my bill totaled sixteen thousand. And that's not counting interest." He took a sip of coffee. "Turns out they'd forgotten to add interment fees and the cost of the headstone along with a couple of other things they said I couldn't live without. I thought that was a pretty interesting way to phrase it."

"So what happened next?"

"What happened next. . ." His voice trailed off. He cleared his throat and continued. "The autopsy results came in. Turned out my wife had overdosed on sleeping pills."

"Oh, Mr. Kratz. I'm so sorry."

He shook his head, and I could see the stiffness in his jaw. "I should've seen it coming. She'd been in so much pain. Tried to tell me she couldn't go on much longer. But I didn't think she would really. . ." His voice broke, and he shifted his gaze to the table. After a bite of the coffee cake, he cleared his throat. "Sorry 'bout that."

"No apologies necessary. You've been through so much."

He nodded but didn't say anything for a moment. "Here's what it comes down to. My wife's life insurance company refused to pay once the coroner ruled her death a suicide. So I've been strapped with monthly payments I can't afford. I'm living on Social Security as it is."

"Do you feel that Eddie Moyer took advantage of you?" I asked.

"His prices are too high," Mr. Kratz said. "That's a given. But there's more to my story than that."

"Ah. Go ahead, please."

I noticed the tightness in his jaw as he continued. "Betty had a beautiful diamond brooch shaped like a flower. It wasn't horribly expensive. I never could give her really nice things, but she'd had it for over thirty years. In the last couple of years, she'd taken to wearing it with a particular blue dress."

"Sounds lovely."

"I asked Eddie Moyer's assistant, Louise, to make sure that Betty was buried with it. I pinned it on that dress myself, just before passing it off to the funeral home. And on the day of her viewing, there it was, for all to see."

"What about the day of the service?" I asked.

"I'd opted for a closed casket," he explained. "And I never thought another thing about that brooch, the day of the funeral, or after, till about a month ago. I'd been struggling to make the payments on the loan, so I decided to pawn a few things. Took my weed eater and an old chain saw to the pawnshop in Groversville. I'd just about finished with my transaction when I happened to notice a showcase filled with antique jewelry. I don't know what made me look closer, but I did."

"And. . . ?" My heart grew heavy as I anticipated his next words.

Roger reached into his pocket and came out with something tightly clutched in his fist. He plopped the diamond brooch on the table, and I gasped.

"You've got to be kidding. He. . .he pawned it?"

"Yes, and that's not all." Betty's wedding ring was there, too. Unfortunately, I didn't have the money to buy it back that day, and the next time I went in, it was gone."

"Oh, Mr. Kratz, this is terrible. Did you go to the police?"

"I tried, but I couldn't prove anything. They said there could be a half dozen pieces of jewelry that looked just like those two. I'd never insured them or anything like that, so there was really no way to prove it. Just my word against Moyer's."

"What about the owner of the pawnshop? Surely he would have a record of who brought it in. Couldn't the police—"

"I asked the owner myself. He said he couldn't remember who'd brought it in. That they'd lost the paperwork. Sounded suspicious to me, but again, what could I do?"

A sick feeling swept over me as I contemplated Roger Kratz's words. Sure, there was the possibility he'd stumbled across the wrong jewels, but the odds of finding both the brooch and the ring. . . ?

"I called Moyer that same day," he said. "And the day after. And the day after. He's denied it, of course, but we both know he's lying."

"Maybe it wasn't Moyer," I offered. "Maybe it was someone else at the funeral home. Someone who would have access and motive." *Like Louise McGillicuddy.*

"Could be." Roger took another large bite of his coffee cake. "Or maybe they're all working together in some sort of underground ring. Though why they need the money from selling jewels of the deceased is a mystery to me, since they're stiffing the customers." He looked at me, and a hint of a smile crossed his lips. "Sorry. Didn't mean it like that."

I smiled, too, as I rethought his words. Suddenly I could hardly wait to share this information with Sheila. She'd found Moyer suspect from the start. Why hadn't I listened to her?

Roger Kratz spent a few more minutes sharing then excused himself, saying he needed to get home to let his dog out. After he left, I took a sip of my too-cool coffee and leaned back in the chair, deep in thought. I wanted to focus on his story, but every time I thought of that blue dress, every time I pondered that brooch, I found myself wondering what dress my husband would choose to bury me in. And what jewels he'd pick to accessorize me. Not that the choices were many.

Folks had always said I looked good in bright colors—purples, reds, blues, that sort of thing. And I had that great red dress I'd worn to Brandi and Scott's wedding in February. Maybe it would do. Of course, it was a little tight these days.

On the other hand, going to meet my Maker in red. . . ? Seemed a bit brazen. Maybe my purple suit would be a better choice. Warren always liked me in purple, and it was a royal color, after all. Perfect for traveling on streets of gold. But what necklace would he choose? And what earrings? Could I really trust Warren with such important decisions? The man didn't even wear matching socks.

Hmm. Maybe I'd better write down all of my preferences, just in case.

"Can I get that for you, ma'am?" The barista jarred me back to reality. He stood next to me, pointing at the empty plates.

"Oh, uh, sure." As he cleaned the table, I noticed some hesitation on his part. "Everything okay?" I asked.

"Yeah, I just wonder about that old guy. Seems a little. . ."

"What?"

"Messed up in the head?"

"Oh?" The kid certainly had my attention now.

"He reminds me of one of those people you hear

about with multiple personalities or something. He was sitting there acting all nice with you. That's not like him. I have to wonder if he switches gears. Like a car. Angry one minute, all nice and sweet the next."

"Well, maybe I just bring out the best in people." I offered up my most convincing smile.

"Maybe." The kid shrugged. "Still, I wouldn't get too close to him, if I were you. He gives me the creeps."

Shaking off my worries, I rose to leave. I needed to take care of one more piece of business while in Wallop—stopping off at the cemetery to search for Sasha. I wouldn't sleep tonight if I didn't give it another shot.

Minutes later I pulled into the parking lot of Moyer's. Passing the funeral home, I made my way down the narrow winding road, hoping to see Jim Roever's cart. No such luck. I searched for what felt like at least an hour for Sasha. Round and round I circled, feeling a bit like a buzzard. At one point I thought I saw something, but it turned out to be a squirrel scampering by.

As I rounded the turn to a familiar portion of the cemetery, my throat began to tighten. It wasn't just about Sasha. I knew that. Pulling off the road, I slipped the car into park and stared in silence at the row of headstones in front of me. I'd avoided this far too long.

Working up the courage to get out of the car was tougher than I expected. So was taking the first few steps. But when I arrived at Judy Blevins's graveside, all of my preconceived notions about death slipped away.

I dropped to my knees and brushed the dirt from her headstone. Read the date of her birth and the date of her death. Contemplated the dash in between.

Then, with tears flowing, I turned my attention to my own dash.

9

I Never Promised You a Rose Garden

On Wednesday afternoon at four o'clock, several of the church ladies met in the courtyard to begin working on the garden. Sheila must've shopped for the occasion. I wasn't sure I'd ever seen her in that particular getup before—a bright floral shirt and denim capris with flower decals on the bottom. Inspirational. Even the pink–and–white tennis shoes were new. And the bright socks.

Evelyn welcomed us and handed out gloves. Then Diedre headed over to the edge of the garden and reached for a frightening-looking contraption.

"This is a tiller," she explained. I marveled that her lyrical brogue made the word "tiller" sound so beautiful. "It's gas-powered, with a two-horsepower engine."

Goodness. You would've thought the woman was showing off a new piece of jewelry.

As the tiller roared to life, we all turned her direction. In that moment, two things occurred to me: (1) You'd have to be quite a woman to handle a two-horsepower tiller, and (2) I'd rather stick with jewels.

Still, Diedre was certainly in her element. She looked like quite the gardening aficionado with that tiller in hand. As she went to work turning the soil with reckless abandon, the rest of us watched in rapt awe, as if we'd somehow stumbled into a movie theater and were privy to a private viewing of an Academy

Award—worthy feature. All we needed was the popcorn and sodas.

Evelyn finally snapped us back to attention. "There are regular shovels, hand shovels, and hoes lining the wall." She pointed to the edge of the courtyard. "If you would each choose your instrument of choice."

She made us sound like an orchestra. I could see it now—the oboes and clarinets warming up. The shovels and hoes playing in tune.

Which instrument should I pick? I hadn't done very well in band, so I decided to start with something relatively easy to operate—a hoe.

Before Sheila reached for a tool, she tossed the gloves Evelyn had given her to the side. Reaching into her pocket, she came out with a pair of the most gorgeous floral gardening gloves I'd ever seen, a real top-of-the-line model.

"Where in the world did you get those?"

"Ordered them off the Internet to protect my nails."

"You got them in less than a week?"

"Mm-hmm. Paid extra." She slipped them on then held up her hands so I could get a better look. Several of the women gathered around, oohing and aahing. "They're leather," Sheila explained. "With extra padding to prevent blisters."

Like Sheila had ever had a blister on her hands.

"The snug wrists are ergonomically designed to give additional support."

Okay, now she sounded like an infomercial. I'd known Sheila most of my adult life and had never—repeat, never—seen the woman in a garden. And now she owned ergonomically designed leather gloves? Had I slipped over into a parallel universe?

"Are they machine washable?" Evelyn asked, drawing near.

"Yep. But you can't put them in the dryer," Sheila cautioned. "I'm supposed to let them dry in the sun. Supposedly doesn't take very long. That way I can get back out into the garden in a jiffy."

Like *that* was going to happen.

Evelyn's face lit with joy. "Well, let's christen those gloves, then!"

She handed Sheila one of the smaller hand shovels, and Sheila looked at it with confusion registering on her face.

"I always say that the best fertilizer is the gardener's shadow." Evelyn spoke above the hum of Diedre's tiller. "So let's get to work, gardeners!"

We divided into areas and began to work at stirring up the soil. Sheila continued to examine her shovel with a perplexed look. "This thing doesn't have much of a handle. Does that mean I have to. . ." She looked at the ground. "Get down on my knees?"

"Mm-hmm."

"In my new pants?" Her wide eyes reflected her surprise at this revelation.

"Yep." I gave her a wink.

"Well, terrific," she muttered. "Just about the time I think things can't get any lower, someone hands me a shovel." She examined it more closely. "It's a pity they didn't tell me what to do with it."

Instead of dropping to her knees as I expected, Sheila meandered from person to person, striking up one conversation after another. Yep. She'd always been great at tilling the soil. That hadn't changed.

Eventually she returned to the spot beside me, eased her way down to the ground, and actually pointed the top of the hand shovel at the earth. Minutes later, above the sound of the motorized tiller, I heard her huffing and puffing. I paused to look her way. "Everything okay?"

"Yeah." She wiped her brow with the back of her arm. "Don't mind me. I'm just getting in touch with my inner green thumb. How about you?"

As I opened my mouth to respond, a disgusting odor suddenly permeated the air. "What in the world is that?"

I looked over to see Diedre and Evelyn opening large bags of something dark brown. "Dirt, maybe?" After another quick sniff, I had to conclude it must be something else entirely. They spread it around and began to work it into the soil, tilling once more.

I gave my nose a pinch, hoping to ease the smell. No such luck. "Those two sure act like they know what they're doing," I observed.

"I'm not sure I'd want to be known for my fertilizing skills." Sheila gave me a wink and got back to work.

I did my best to focus on the task at hand and, after awhile, found myself enjoying the steady rhythm of the hoe against the ground. For whatever reason, tilling the soil got me to thinking about the mystery surrounding Fiona's death. Had I dug deep enough in my conversation with Roger Kratz? Was he hiding evidence just under the surface, perhaps? And what about Louise McGillicuddy? Why did the woman make me uneasy?

These and a thousand other thoughts rolled around in my brain as I worked. Finally, as my imagination took over, I reminded myself that we didn't even know if Fiona had been murdered. Maybe I'd been wasting my time focusing on. . .what was it the Bible called them again? Ah yes. . .vain imaginings. Instead of fretting over the unknown, I should've taken advantage of my "tilling time" to pray and thank God for the people who were still here.

In the middle of my ponderings, Janetta appeared, clapping her hands to get our attention. "Ladies, it's nearly time to come inside for snacks. I can't wait to show you what I've been working on."

"Diedre and I will do a brief teaching after our meal," Evelyn reminded us.

"Great," Sheila leaned over and muttered. "Dinner *and* a show."

After finishing up in the courtyard, we headed to the fellowship hall, pausing in the ladies' room to scrub up.

"That wasn't half bad," I admitted as I washed the dirt from my arms. Rubbing at my shoulder, I added, "But I'll bet I'm sore tomorrow."

"Me, too." Sheila dried her hands then examined them. She held them up for my approval. "Not one blister."

"Great gloves."

"Some things are worth paying extra for."

I wanted to add, "Just not an ergonomically de-signed preplanned funeral service, eh?" but opted not to. No point in spoiling a nice moment.

We joined the others in the fellowship hall and filled our plates with some of the most delicious-looking food I'd ever seen. I had to admit, Janetta had outdone herself this time. She'd done up some beautiful veggie wraps—very colorful and filled with flavor. The cream cheese gave it that extra oomph that every wrap needs. We all ate like we might never see food again.

Afterward, Evelyn and Diedre took their places in the front of the room. The knees of Diedre's slacks were stained, and her face glowed with that "I've just spent the afternoon in the sun" look, but she smiled and greeted us with great enthusiasm. "Thanks for all your hard work today, ladies, and thanks to Janetta for putting together that delicious meal. I think we all owe her a round of applause."

Janetta's cheeks reddened as we cheered.

Evelyn finally got us calmed down. "Ladies, we appreciate the fact that you trust us enough to let us deviate from our usual Wednesday night schedule. I'm sure your families missed having dinner with you tonight, but I felt it was important to share a meal together."

I smiled, knowing that Warren and Devin had eaten dinner at Lee Yu's Garden, the restaurant that Brandi managed, and were probably pulling up to the church for their usual classes. Somehow I doubted they'd missed me, at least much.

"This Bible study will be different from anything we've ever done," Evelyn explained. "For one thing, Diedre's going to be doing much of the teaching. This is a first for her, so give her your full, undivided attention."

Evelyn took her seat, and Diedre took over. "Thank you for allowing me this privilege. I told you that tonight's teaching would be called 'Consider a Field.' What I didn't tell you was. . .that field is your heart."

Oh my.

"The Proverbs 31 woman loved the Lord and loved her family," Diedre explained, "and that showed in her every action. But in order to love the Lord wholeheartedly and to care for our families in the way she did, we must allow God to do a complete work in our hearts."

I thought about that for a minute. I'd given my heart to the Lord years ago. Had settled the salvation issue when I was just a child. And He'd done plenty of work in my heart since. Still, with all the turmoil surrounding Fiona's death, I'd struggled with a few private heart issues.

"I want to start by talking about the soil we tilled in the courtyard," Diedre continued. "It might just be dirt to us, but to the flowers we're going to plant, the soil is home. A place to live. And preparing it is critical. The flowers won't thrive if we put them in unprepared soil. If we don't take the time to get the ground ready, anything we plant in it will surely die. . .in time. That's why we worked so hard and why we added the manure."

"Disgusting," Sheila whispered. "Do we have to talk about this on a full stomach?"

"In so many ways, our hearts are like that ground out there," Diedre explained. "Hard. Crusted over. It takes the rain, kind of like the little shower we had on Monday, to soften things up. Problem is, sometimes we don't want to be softened. Sometimes we get set in our ways. Don't want anything to change."

I groaned inwardly.

"Then along comes God," Diedre continued. "With that spiritual tiller of His, digging right down to the places we don't want to expose."

Oh dear.

"The Bible says we are to bear fruit, to live productive lives. But that's not possible if we don't allow God to prepare our hearts, just like we prepared that soil out there today. I daresay, He's got a little digging to do."

Um, a little?

"In order for Him to do this work, we've got to be willing to draw near to Him. To come into His presence. It might seem a bit frightening to think about for some of us. Likely some of us were raised to believe that God was in the business of slapping us down when we failed. But that's not true."

Thank You, Lord.

Diedre opened her Bible. "I want to share a scripture from Exodus, chapter three, verse five: 'Do not come any closer,' God said. 'Take off your sandals, for the place where you are standing is holy ground.' " She looked up with a smile. "It's hard for me to imagine God speaking to Moses out of a burning bush. Must have been quite an overwhelming experience."

At this point, her eyes filled with tears. "Every time you see that garden out there, I want you to be reminded that whenever you come into God's presence, whenever you draw near to Him and allow Him to work on your heart, you're standing on holy ground, just like Moses. It might be a strange and even terrifying experience to draw that close, but He wants to get to the deep and hidden places in your heart. He wants you to know that you're safe in His presence. He longs to spend time with you—not to slap you down, but to work through the problems and to strengthen you.

"And speaking of which. . ." She clapped her hands together. "Let's get into small groups. Spend some time sharing. Then get alone with the Lord and ask Him to search your heart. Ask Him to show you the places where you've grown hard. Stubborn. Give Him permission to till the soil, to soften you up so you're ready for seed planting."

Goodness, this woman was good. We divided into groups, and I found myself teamed up with Janetta, Evelyn, and Candy, who must've slipped in just after the teaching started. Evelyn kicked us off with a group prayer, and then Janetta went first, her eyes filling with tears.

"I had no idea this would be so difficult." She brushed at her eyes with the back of her hand. "I'm just a baby Christian. Only been walking with the Lord eight months, so I still have a lot to learn. I'm sure no Proverbs 31 woman, at least not yet. But this whole thing about letting God soften my heart. . ." She shook her head and put a hand on her chest, as if to somehow protect the broken places inside. "There's a lot of unfinished business inside of me. I guess it's finally time to let the Lord dig into the hidden places. I hope I'm up for this."

I could relate. After all that had happened over the past couple of weeks, my heart was in need of a good "tilling." As the women huddled together around Janetta as she poured out her heart, I reached for my Bible and turned to the passage from Exodus that Diedre had referred to. I read it again then looked up into Janetta's tear-filled eyes as reality hit.

We were truly standing. . .or in this case, sitting. . . on holy ground.

10

I Went to a Garden Party

On Saturday afternoon, Candy and I drove to Janetta's house to finalize the catering plans for the wedding. Brandi had hoped to come along to lend moral support but couldn't get away from the restaurant, so we agreed to gather the Peterson and Caine clans at Lee Yu's Garden for dinner at six. It was about time we all got together for some quality prewedding celebrating. In the meantime, we wanted to hear Janetta's final thoughts on the food for Candy and Garrett's courtyard reception. What sorts of goodies had she cooked up to tempt our palates?

We arrived at her house—the official home of Clark County Catering—at four thirty on the dot. Janetta's son, Jake, met us at the door with a broad smile on his face. Of course he had a lot to smile about these days. From what Janetta had told me on the phone that morning, he'd just proposed to his girlfriend, Nikki, and she'd accepted. Looked like Clarksborough would stay in wedding-planning mode for a good long while.

Candy greeted Jake with a smile and an enthusiastic "Congratulations!"

"We heard your good news this morning," I added. "When's the big day?"

"October," he said. "We met in the fall, so Nikki thought it would be appropriate to get married then."

Candy nodded in my direction. "Well, if you need anyone to help plan the wedding, my mom's the best. And she's the one who got you two together, anyway."

Well, that was one way to put it. It was good of Candy not to mention that I'd once suspected Jake and Nikki of robbing the Clark County Savings and Loan. Of course, that was a lifetime ago. Hopefully they'd forgiven me for my little faux pas.

Jake ushered us inside, and we worked our way through the house till we arrived at the oversized kitchen, where we found Janetta decorating a birthday cake.

I whistled as I took in the amazing cake. It looked like a castle, complete with turrets and a miniature moat made out of sugar.

"Cinderella birthday party for a seven-year-old," Janetta explained. "Tomorrow afternoon at 2:00."

"Lucky kid." I gave the cake a thorough examination, marveling at the little horse and carriage she'd placed in front. "You just get better all the time, Janetta. You made all of this?"

"Yeah." She smiled. The horses are made from fondant. Aren't they adorable?"

"They're magnificent."

Her cheeks flushed pink as she thanked me. "I love helping people plan for their celebrations." She turned to look at Candy. "And I can't tell you when I've been this excited about a wedding." Her sparkling eyes reflected her joy.

"Me either!" Candy giggled.

"I love the whole garden party theme. And those daisies!" Janetta went off on a tangent, bragging about

Candy's floral choices. "The bright colors in those gerbera daisies you brought by a couple of weeks ago were the basis for my menu choices. Hot pink, orange, yellow. . .talk about a feast for the eyes! I want to match it with a feast for the stomach."

Candy's face beamed. "Can you show us what you've come up with?"

"Of course!" Janetta wiped the frosting from her hands and took a seat at the table, gesturing for us to do the same. As Candy leaned in close, I noticed the excitement in her eyes. She and Janetta were a matched set.

Hmm. For some reason, the words "matched set" got me to thinking about Sasha and Copper. Thinking about Sasha and Copper got me to thinking about my trip to the cemetery the other day. Thinking about my trip to the cemetery got me to thinking about Roger Kratz. And thinking about Roger Kratz got me to thinking about cinnamon-swirl coffee cake. All of which somehow got me back around to thinking about Janetta and the food for Candy's wedding.

Yep. You really could function in the real world with ADD.

"You had such great ideas the last time we met." Janetta gave Candy an encouraging smile. "So I just built on those. Here's what I'm thinking. . ." She opened a yellow tablet, and my eyes widened at how much I saw written there. Thank goodness Warren had already paid her in advance. Otherwise I'd be plenty nervous right about now.

"Let's start by talking about the appetizer table." Janetta pointed to the top of the page. "This will be the first table your guests see as they arrive in the courtyard. Playing off the colors in the daisies, I plan to do some gorgeous fruit trays with all sorts of seasonal goodies. Really pretty stuff. I'll also arrange some of the fruit in vases to look like flowers. I think you're going to be stunned when you see what can be done with the chocolate-covered strawberries. And pineapple can be cut to look like daisies. You just have to use maraschino cherries cut in half for their middles. I've been practicing."

"Yum. Sounds perfect." Candy's face beamed.

"I'll do vegetable trays, too, of course," Janetta continued. "I plan to cut many of the veggies to look like flowers. They're going to be amazing."

Sounded like a lot of trouble to me.

"I'm pretty good at cutting carrots into flower shapes," she explained. "I've also been practicing on zucchini flowers and decorative cucumber twirls and celery curls. And did you know that you can cut radishes to look like roses?"

"Um, no." *But I'll file that away.*

She showed us a picture, and I had to admit, they were very. . .floral.

"To finish off the appetizer table, we'll have a variety of cheeses and crackers. I managed to track down some crackers shaped like flowers. And I'll use my miniature cookie cutters to shape the cheese like daisies. . .don't worry about that."

Like I would worry.

"Oh, and dip," Janetta continued. "I was thinking spinach."

She looked down at her tablet then back up at us, her face beaming. "Now for the good stuff—the main table. I plan to use cookie cutters to make hundreds of small flower-shaped sandwiches. They'll have a variety of meat and cheese fillings, everything from turkey and Swiss to ham and cheddar to cucumber and cream cheese with dill. And I'll use toothpicks to fasten cherry tomatoes in the center of each sandwich," she said. "That way they'll look more like real flowers."

Where did the woman come up with these things?

"We'll also have chicken salad on croissants, spinach and bacon quiche—the tiny petite-sized ones—baked in floral-shaped tins, festive pasta salad, cucumber salad, and Asian coleslaw with cabbage, ramen noodles, sesame seeds, and almonds."

Man, was I getting hungry. "Sounds like a lot of food."

"Well, you're expecting 350 guests, right?"

"True." I nodded.

"And not everyone will eat the same things. That's why it's a great idea to offer such a wide variety, especially with finger foods."

"This all sounds so tempting," Candy said with an admiring smile. "I skipped lunch today."

"Me, too. I'll probably eat the entire buffet at Lee Yu's Garden this evening." I chuckled, envisioning what *that* would look like.

"Oh!" Janetta snapped back to attention. "I almost forgot. You haven't even heard the best part yet. Let's talk about the sweets table."

Images of my dimpled thighs resurfaced at once.

Janetta pointed at the bottom of the yellow-lined page. "I know we talked about having a chocolate fountain. I was thinking white chocolate, since we're doing a summertime theme. What do you think of that?"

"Sounds great." Candy nodded in agreement. "What will you use for dipping?"

"Oh, a host of things. . .wedding cookies, pretzels, marshmallows, honey graham sticks, fruit. Strawberries are great for dipping in chocolate, as I mentioned before. Pineapple, too. And cherries."

I felt my blood sugar rising as she spoke. My head began to swim as I contemplated the chocolate fountain. Chances were pretty good that I would put on ten pounds during the afternoon of the wedding. I'd have to warn Warren in advance to steer me away from the sweets table, at least until after the guests had gone.

"I've done a sketch of the wedding cake." Janetta flipped the page in the notepad. Candy and I gasped as we eyed the picture of the beautiful three-tiered cake topped with silk daisies. They flowed down one whole side of the cake in a colorful array and wrapped around the front, which made the whole thing come alive with color.

"Oh, Janetta!" Candy's eyes filled with tears. "It's even prettier than I imagined."

"Aw, you're making me blush." Janetta paused to smile. "I was blessed to find those flower-shaped pans. I think they make all the difference in the world and give me an opportunity to really make the most of the Gerber daisy theme."

"You've done that all right," Candy said.

Janetta's cheeks turned crimson. "I just wanted to

double-check flavors. You said white cake, right? With cream cheese frosting and raspberry filling?"

"Mm-hmm."

I think she must've lost Candy at the words "raspberry filling." My daughter's eyes took on a glassy look. Diabetic coma, likely. There was something about sweets that tended to send us Petersons into a catatonic state. In a good way. My stomach suddenly began to rumble, and I could hardly wait to get to the restaurant. All this talk about food was really getting to me.

Oblivious to my ponderings, Janetta continued on. "We will have a table for drinks," she explained. "Regular tea, Mango tea, and raspberry-lemonade punch, like you suggested the last time we met. I'll make sure to have plenty of sliced lemons on hand. I've got the best technique for curling them." She paused for breath then dove in again. "Oh, and we'll have coffee, of course, with a variety of flavored creamers." She picked up her pen and turned to Candy. "Did I leave anything out?"

"Are you kidding me?" My daughter gave her an admiring whistle. "Janetta, you're a pro. I can't believe you've spent this much time putting together a plan for my wedding reception. You're. . .amazing."

"Well, my kids will help me," she explained. "They love being in this business with me, and I enjoy working with them, too."

"Still, it's a lot of work," I said. "When do you sleep?"

Janetta gave me a funny look. "What do you mean?"

"I mean, you're such a go-getter. You must've worked round the clock to come up with all of this."

"Oh, well, I. . ."

"You. . .and Evelyn. . .and Diedre. You're all. . . amazing. Don't you ever let me catch you saying you're not a Proverbs 31 woman again. You are, in every sense of the word."

"Oh, Annie. . ." Janetta's eyes filled with tears. "This kind of work comes naturally to me, just like editing does to you." She dabbed at her eyes. "And crime-fighting. I daresay you're far better at that than I'll ever be at cooking."

"Somehow I doubt it." I chuckled. "I can absolutely assure you, my editing clients will never go away feeling as happy—or as full—as your clients. And I've never dipped a suspect in chocolate before, white, semisweet, or otherwise. You're a whiz, Janetta. Truly."

Her cheeks flushed pink. "I can't tell you how much that means to me." She reached across the table and squeezed my hand. She might as well have been squeezing my heart. Tears rose to my lashes immediately, and I wrapped my fingers around hers, thanking God for such a wonderful friend.

We wrapped up our meeting in short order, and Candy called Garrett to come pick her up so they could stop off at the deejay's house to drop off yet another check on the way to the restaurant.

Garrett arrived at Janetta's house within minutes. I looked at my handsome son-in-law-to-be and smiled as he wrapped Candy in his arms. They complemented each other perfectly. His tall, broad-shouldered stature seemed the perfect match to her petite and slender one. They fit together like puzzle pieces.

Seeing the two of them made me think of Warren.

As I climbed into my car, I decided to give him a call. He answered with a smile in his voice. I always loved it when that happened.

"Are you coming by the house to pick me up?" he asked.

"I'll be there in about ten minutes. I'm starved."

"Me, too."

"What have you been up to this afternoon?" I queried.

"Just hanging out with Copper. I taught him to roll over. And now we're working on playing dead."

"No way." First of all, I had a hard time picturing Warren deliberately spending time with the dog that, until a few days ago, had driven him stark-raving mad. Second, I had a hard time imagining Copper actually obeying.

"We're having fun." Warren called out to Copper, and I could hear panting in the background.

"Well, I'll be there shortly, so you'd better teach him how to not chew on the sofa while we're away."

"We're working on that."

As we ended the call, my thoughts shifted, once again, to Sasha. As much as I'd grown to love Copper, I missed my baby girl terribly. In that frame of mind, I decided to telephone Moyer's to see if I could track down Jim Roever. Had he seen my little darling?

The phone rang several times, and no one answered. I glanced at my watch and realized that they were probably closed.

Just as I reached the "I'm going to hang up" point, a brusque voice came on the line. "Hello?"

"Um, hello. This is Annie Peterson, calling about Sasha."

"Excuse me? Who?"

I recognized Louise McGillicuddy's voice, but she sounded. . .odd. Like she'd been crying, perhaps. *Why the tears, Louise?*

"Annie Peterson," I reminded her. "My friend Sheila and I came in last week to talk with Mr. Moyer about prepaid funeral plans. Then afterward, we—"

"Ah. Of course. How can I help you, Mrs. Peterson?"

"I'm looking for Jim Roever. We talked after my last visit. He's been helping me look for—"

"Jim Roever is no longer employed by Moyer's."

"W–what?"

"Mr. Moyer let him go last week."

Let him go? "Would you mind. . .I mean, would it be possible to get his number?"

"I'm sorry, but I can't give out personal information for any of our employees."

But he's not an employee. . .anymore.

"Have a nice day." And with that, Louise McGilli-cuddy clicked off.

I closed my phone and focused on the road ahead. Jim Roever had been fired. Coincidence. . .or something more?

As I pulled into our driveway, I contemplated the news from every angle. Why would Eddie Moyer fire one of his employees right after someone died on their property? Had Jim Roever somehow been involved in Fiona's death? Or. . .

Perhaps Roever was the one who'd been stealing jewels from the deceased. Yes, that made perfect sense. Likely Moyer had caught him red-handed and fired him on the spot.

A shiver ran down my spine as this possibility registered. Perhaps the kindhearted caretaker wasn't so kindhearted after all. Maybe, just maybe, he'd been doing more than planting flowers. Maybe he'd been planting stolen jewels. . .in pawn shops all over Clark County and beyond.

Only one way to know for sure. . . Looked like I needed to do a little digging.

Where, oh, where was that two-horsepower tiller when I needed it?

11

STOP. . .AND SMELL THE ROSES

Warren and I entered Lee Yu's Garden at six o'clock. I looked around, amazed at the crowd. "Wow. Hope Brandi saved a table for us."

"I did."

I turned as I heard my oldest daughter's voice. "Well, hey there." I wrapped her in a warm hug. "Working hard or hardly working?"

She gestured to the noisy restaurant. "Which do you think?"

I gave her a wink then paused to look at the large room filled with happy customers. The three buffet areas were surrounded on every side by people, young and old. From here, I could see the plates, which filled with food. And the smell! "Mmm." I could almost taste the BBQ spareribs now. "You've really done a great job in turning this place around, honey." I flashed an encouraging smile. "I remember when Lee Yu's Garden hardly did any business. And now. . ."

"Now it's the hottest place in town." She laughed. "Hotter than a plate of Szechuan chicken."

"And hotter than usual today," I added, fanning myself. "Can you believe this weather?"

"It's never this warm in May," Brandi agreed. "I don't think I was prepared for it. The high temperatures are really getting to me."

That would explain why she looked so exhausted.

Well, that and the mob of people.

Brandi ushered us into a private room off on the side of the restaurant, where we found the others in our group waiting. "The party can start now," Warren announced to the group as we made our entrance. I looked over at my husband, my heart swelling with joy. Oh, how I loved him. He always made everyone feel so happy and comfortable. Truly a gift.

Diedre and her husband, Patrick, waved from the far end of the table. I smiled in her direction, and Warren went over to shake Patrick's hand. Candy and Garrett signaled for me and Brandi to join them. I met my daughter with a huge hug, determined to press all thoughts of the investigation out of my mind altogether. Tonight was her night.

"Where's Devin?" I looked around, confused by my son's absence. He'd been looking forward to dinner with the family, or so I thought.

Candy winked. "He has a date tonight. Last-minute."

"A date? Are you serious?"

"One of the girls from the debate team," Brandi added. "He asked her out on a whim."

I looked back and forth between my two daughters. "So both of you knew?"

"What? About Devin's date with that girl from the debate team?" Warren sat in the chair next to me, and I turned to him, astounded.

"You knew, too?"

"He called me while you were at Janetta's," Warren explained. "I think he was afraid you would. . ."

"What?"

"Well, you tend to get all worked up when things

don't go well." Warren spoke softly.

Though a pang of jealousy ripped through me, I forced myself not to knee-jerk. So Devin had told everyone except me. *Hmm.* Possibly because he knew me too well. Knew I'd ask too many questions. Knew I'd be disappointed if he ended up with a broken heart, as was often the case.

I drew in a deep breath and counted to ten. Silently. After that, I deliberately shifted my focus to Diedre, telling her how much I'd enjoyed her teaching last Wednesday. She responded with a glowing smile and a happy "It's just the Lord" response.

I looked up as her oldest son, Sean, entered the room. He took a seat next to Garrett, and they dove into a conversation about a baseball game they'd just watched. Within minutes, Brandi's husband, Scott, entered. I hadn't seen nearly enough of Brandi and Scott over the past few weeks, but from his beaming face, I figured he must be enjoying married life.

He stopped by my chair and gave me a hug. "Good to see you, Mom."

"You, too." I gave him a warm smile then turned to Garrett—my soon-to-be son-in-law. Not that he noticed. No, his gaze was fixed on Candy, as was usually the case. I'd never seen a man so smitten, and that made me smile from the inside out. In just three short weeks he would join the family. He might not be the prankster Scott was, but Garrett seemed to fit in with the Peterson clan just fine.

I paused for a moment to reflect on the word *clan.* The Caines were a true clan in every sense of the word. I hadn't done much research on the Petersons to know what, exactly, we were. Perhaps I'd have to borrow Sheila's ergonomically designed gloves and do a bit of digging to find out. Regardless, we were family—and a happy one, at that. Soon to be larger, once Garrett joined us.

My heart lurched as Brandi let out an ear-piercing whistle, something she'd learned from her father. "Everyone ready to eat?"

A dizzying chorus of positive responses followed.

We headed through the crowd to the buffet, where I tried to pick the least fattening foods to fill my plate. After all that talk about sweets this afternoon, I could feel the pounds coming on, so I reminded myself to be careful.

As soon as we returned to the table and prayed together, Candy got our attention. "I know we're supposed to be relaxing tonight," she announced, "but if you're all okay with this, I'd like to go over our plans for the wedding. It's so hard to get all of us together that I want to take advantage of the situation. Does anyone mind?"

"Of course not." Diedre and I spoke in unison.

"As long as I can still eat," Warren said, reaching for his fork.

Candy pulled out a notebook—one that looked eerily like my supersleuthing notebook—and began to read from her notes. If this girl wasn't a chip off the old block, I didn't know who was.

"The wedding rehearsal will take place on Friday night, June third, at seven o'clock, with a rehearsal dinner following here at Lee Yu's Garden."

Out of the corner of my eye, I noticed that Brandi beamed at that announcement. She'd suggested it, after all, and had even planned the menu.

Candy continued, with zeal lacing every word. "On the day of the wedding, the girls will be getting ready at my parents' house—we're meeting at ten o'clock to have brunch before working on hair and makeup—and the guys will get ready at the Caines' place. Garrett can fill you in on the time. Girls will caravan to the church at one and meet in the prayer chapel just off the sanctuary. Guys will meet in the room where the men have their midweek Bible study. The ceremony will start at two."

"Garrett, have all your groomsmen committed to be here in time for the ceremony?" Diedre flashed a concerned look. I knew they were worried that Garrett's college roommate might be out of the country on a missions-related project.

I hadn't lost much sleep over this problem. After all, the bridal party was the largest I'd ever heard of—eight bridesmaids, eight groomsmen, a junior brides-maid, a flower girl, and a ring bearer. There would be little room left at the front of the church for the bride, the groom, and the pastor.

"I'm still not sure about Joe," Garrett assured us. "But if he's able to come, he'll fly in the night before. I've already arranged for him to be picked up in Philly at the airport."

For some reason, when I heard the word "Philly," my thoughts shifted to Maggie Preston. I wondered—for the second or third time, actually—why she'd gone off to Philadelphia on the day of Fiona's death. I hadn't come out and asked her, had I? Perhaps I should.

Annie, stay focused. You're not supposed to be thinking about that tonight.

"Garrett and I have already met with Pastor Miller and given him the order of service," Candy continued. "And here's some fun news. We've hired a string quartet and a harpist."

"You have?" I turned to her, stunned. How come I didn't know this?

"Don't worry, Mom." Candy gave me a relaxed smile. "This is something Garrett's mom wanted to do for us as a wedding gift. She thought it would be beautiful for the whole garden theme, and I agree."

"Wow." I nodded in Diedre's direction. The woman never ceased to amaze me. She'd probably turn out to be the harpist.

"Back to the wedding." Candy smiled. "After the service, we'll send the guests out to the courtyard area for appetizers while the photographer takes our pictures. The string quartet will provide background music for our guests, so hopefully they won't miss us too much. After the photographer has finished—and I've given him strict instructions that the photography session can't last more than twenty minutes—we'll all end up together for the most beautiful garden party reception you've ever seen."

We all agreed that her plans sounded wonderful. Detailed, but wonderful.

As we emptied our plates, we all responded to Candy's description of the big day with enthusiastic comments. Between bites, of course.

I was just about to go back to the buffet for seconds when a familiar voice rang out. "Did you start the party without me?"

I looked up, surprised to see Devin standing in the

doorway. "But I thought. . ."

Candy gave me a "Mom, don't say it" look, and I clammed up. My son might be putting on a happy face, but it was only for our benefit. That girl from the debate team had broken his heart; I knew it.

We made our way through the crowd to the buffet once again. I noticed that Devin loaded up his plate with an assortment of high-calorie, high-carb goodies. I hated to say the boy was drowning his sorrows in food, but the facts were difficult to dispute.

After we filled our plates and returned to the table, a memory resurfaced. I'd told Maggie that Devin might be interested in working at the florist's shop. I broached the subject carefully. "I, um, I hear that Maggie Preston's having a hard time keeping up with things at the shop."

"Oh?" He gave me an inquisitive look.

"Yes, she's pretty swamped. Needs to hire someone before summer kicks in. Said she'd be willing to train him. Or her." I paused and looked around the table, hoping to plant a few seeds in my son's mind. "Know anyone who's looking to make a little extra money?"

I'm so clever. Devin's been telling me for weeks that he needs a part-time job after graduation. I offered an encouraging smile.

"What would the person have to do?"

I turned as I heard an unexpected voice on my left. Sean. "W—what?"

"Is she looking for someone to tend to the nursery out back or someone to arrange flowers?" he asked. "I've had experience with both and need some part-time work while I wrap up my master's."

Diedre's face lit up. "Oh, this is a fabulous idea! I don't know why I didn't think of it myself. Why, Sean was practically raised in my garden, and he used to help Fiona in her nursery on the weekends. He'd be perfect to help Maggie."

I couldn't help the sigh that escaped. I felt like my balloon had deflated, right there for everyone to see.

"I would offer, too," Diedre said, "but I'm so busy at the gym."

Another sigh slipped out. Diedre taught an aerobics class at the Clark County Coed Fitness Center on Main. I knew, because I was supposed to be in it. Key words: "supposed to be."

"And besides," Diedre continued, "these Wednesday evening classes at the church are taking quite of a bit of my time, as well." She turned to her son with a reassuring nod. "But Sean here is certainly at home with flowers. He's got the greenest thumb of any Irishman I ever knew." She laughed at her own joke, and her husband and sons joined in.

"My mom always gets a kick out of that one," Garrett whispered in my ear. "She thinks it's a nice coincidence that the Caines all have green thumbs."

Speaking of green thumbs got me to thinking about Jim Roever. Thinking about Jim Roever reminded me of Louise McGillicuddy's startling news today on the phone about his dismissal. Thinking of that news made me wonder about Roger Kratz and his wife's brooch. Thinking about the brooch shifted my thoughts to Eddie Moyer. Did he fire Roever because of the pawned jewels, or had he done the dirty deed himself? How would I ever figure this out?

"Are you with us, Annie?" Warren gave me a funny look.

"Mm-hmm." I was at Lee Yu's Garden. . .in body.

Diedre carried on, talking about the garden. I tried to pay attention but found it difficult. My thoughts would not be stilled. And why should they be, after all? The whole world had gone crazy. Fiona Kelly was dead. Sasha was missing. Maggie Preston was noticeably absent from the flower shop. Louise McGillicuddy was all choked up. . .about something. Roger Kratz suspected Eddie Moyer of pawning jewels. Jim Roever had been fired. Eddie Moyer wore fine Italian suits and charged far too much for funeral services. Diedre had a green thumb. Evelyn had great upper arms. Janetta Mullins could carve radishes into roses. Sheila had ergonomically designed gloves. My husband was teaching the dog to do tricks. I hardly got to see my oldest daughter anymore. My second daughter was about to get married. And Devin's heart had probably been broken again.

All of these things in combination were suddenly too much to take. With the sweet-and-sour sauce still fresh on my lips, I excused myself from the table and went to the ladies' room. . .to deal with some unexpected tears.

12

CONSIDER THE LILIES

On Sunday morning I awoke with new resolve. Likely last night's tears were due to a combination of things: exhaustion, premenopause, and wedding planning, to name a few. I needed to slow down. Take things easy. Pay more attention to the things that mattered and less to my own shortcomings. Stop comparing myself to others. Get God's perspective on my situation.

I started the morning by reading my Bible, focusing on the issue of insecurity, which had, of late, taken hold. I wanted to know if the Proverbs 31 woman ever struggled with it, so I started there. My gaze fell on the twenty-fifth verse. "She is clothed with strength and dignity; she can laugh at the days to come."

Hmm. I hadn't been laughing much last night, had I? And lately it felt as if all my strength had been zapped. I'd allowed fear, both of aging and of my own mortality, to rob me of that. And dignity? I sighed as I realized the truth: My insecurities had nearly stripped it away.

Sensing that the Lord had some tilling to do, I thumbed to the New Testament, where I stumbled across a familiar scripture in the sixth chapter of Matthew: "'See how the lilies of the field grow. They do not labor or spin. Yet I tell you that not even Solomon in all his splendor was dressed like one of these.'"

I knew the inference, of course—that God would care for my every need. But today I saw this scripture in a new light. Lilies were beautiful in God's eyes. . . every single one of them. He didn't look at a field of flowers and say that one was prettier—or better—than the other. No, each was splendiferous.

I pondered something Janetta had said yesterday afternoon about Candy's daisies. She didn't say, "The pink one is prettier than the orange," or "The yellow one really grabbed my attention." No, it was the combination of all the colors that impacted her. She remembered them. . .as a whole. Vibrant. Beautiful. All merged together as one unit.

Surely when God looked at the women in my circle of friends: me, Sheila, Diedre, Evelyn, Janetta, and so forth, He didn't say, "Oh, that Evelyn is a brighter shade than Annie," or vice versa. Likely His take on things was much the same as Janetta's. He saw us as a bouquet of flowers, each color adding to the other. I might never know which color daisy I was in the grand scheme of things, but I now realized that my color was critical to the equation. The vase would be incomplete without me.

With that in mind, I thought I'd better stop cutting myself down. Better stop worrying about who was the better cook or who could teach a better Bible study lesson. Who could plant a lovely garden and who could solve a crime. Who could keep her upper arms in good shape and who could carve pineapples into daisies. Who would make the better mother-in-law or aerobics instructor. The Lord needed all of us in His garden. And as much as He needed us, we needed Him even more.

Still in a gardening frame of mind, I went in search of another scripture from the Song of Solomon. "My lover has gone down into his garden, to the beds of spices, to browse in the gardens, and to gather lilies."

In a wild rush of imagination, I pictured the Lord walking through a field, reaching down to gather up a bouquet of lilies—His children—into His hands. I could almost see Him now, reaching down to pick me up, cradling me close, and telling me how much He loved me, how much He valued me simply for. . . being. Not doing.

In that moment, as the realization hit, I breathed a huge sigh of relief. If I never solved another crime, if my wedding-planning skills disappeared altogether, if all my earthly talents flew away on the next wind, I would still be lovely to God. It wasn't about what I did or didn't do. He didn't need me to impress Him, and neither did my friends. What He needed. . .what they all needed. . .was my love.

Relief flooded over me as I prayed about these things. No longer did I have to fret over how people viewed me. There was no point in trying to keep up with the Joneses. I was a beautiful flower to my heavenly Father.

That thought stayed with me as Warren and I headed off to church, where Pastor Miller spoke on the topic of joy. It remained with me all throughout the afternoon as our family gathered together for lunch and board games afterward. It lingered in my mind as I sat on the couch later that evening, Warren on one side, Copper on the other, a bowl of Moo-lennium Crunch ice cream in my hands. It planted itself firmly in my thoughts as I dressed for bed and as Warren and I cuddled together with Copper curled up at our feet. It danced through my memory as we talked about how our lives were changing now that the kids were growing up. And it spoke in gentle whispers as I drifted off to sleep on Sunday night.

By the time I awoke Monday morning, I felt invincible. No, I didn't have to prove anything. I suddenly felt energized to work as never before. Not so that people would take notice of me, but for my own personal satisfaction.

After my quiet time, I opened an e-mail attachment from a client and started editing her manuscript. The same joy that Pastor Miller spoke about the previous day stuck with me as I zipped through the first three chapters of her book. After that, I responded to several e-mails then telephoned my mother in Mississippi to find out when she and my father would arrive for the wedding. Something about hearing her voice brought a smile to my face. With that done, I placed a call to the wedding photographer then checked in with Brandi to finalize plans for the rehearsal dinner.

After all of that, I shifted gears. It was time to get back to work on another project, one I'd put off all weekend.

For the past twenty-four hours, I'd toyed with the idea of telephoning Jim Roever. I just couldn't seem to let go of the idea. Sure, I wanted to know why he'd been fired. But something else had been bothering me, as well.

If Jim Roever had been stealing jewels, maybe he'd stolen something else, too.

Sasha.

Maybe—when he'd seen her slip through that crack in the window—he'd made a decision to kidnap her. My mind reeled at the very idea. Why he'd want her, I wasn't sure. Sure, she could get into small spaces. She was a born hunter, after all. But why would a cemetery caretaker turned jewel thief need a dog?

For evil purposes, perhaps?

I contemplated the fact that my canine companion might've been pulled over to the dark side. Did she now work for the enemy? Had she switched from crime-solving to a life of crime?

I could hardly fathom it. How would I ever begin to reform her? Did the folks at Coats 'n Tails have an obedience class for doggies gone astray? Would Warren be willing to pay for it?

Don't jump the gun, Annie. First things first. I needed to find her. I punched in the number for information then asked for James Roever in Wallop. Thankfully only one name came up. I breathed a sigh of relief and gave him a call. He answered right away.

"Hello?"

I tried to speak above my nerves. "Mr. Roever? This is Annie Peterson, the lady who lost her dog."

"Of course, Mrs. Peterson. Good to hear from you. Did you ever find her?" His voice sounded. . . compassionate. *Suspicious.* Was Sasha sitting at his side even now? Curled up on the sofa next to him? Eating his treats? Drinking his water? Had Jim Roever—the cad—discovered that my baby liked to sleep under the covers at night and that she wouldn't go outside to do her business when it was raining?

Pay attention, Annie.

"No, I haven't found her yet," I explained. "I was just about to ask you that same question. I went by the cemetery the other day, hoping to find you, but. . ."

"Um, yes. . ." His voice trailed off. "I, um, I'm not employed by Moyer's anymore."

"Yes, I talked to Louise a couple of days ago. She sounded a bit. . .upset."

"I doubt that had anything to do with me. She's been sounding like that ever since Eddie Moyer got married."

"Ah, I see." *So that's it. She has a broken heart.* Suddenly the somber look on her face made perfect sense.

"I tried to tell her years ago not to get involved with Eddie. He's, well, we didn't always see eye to eye. Still, I hated to leave on a bad note, and that's exactly what happened."

"I–I'm so sorry to hear that." *But I'd love to hear more.*

"I'd been thinking of retiring anyway," Roever continued. "I've worked longer than most and wouldn't mind doing a little traveling. It really bothers me that our relationship ended the way it did. I worked for Moyer's when Eddie's father ran the place. Been there thirty-five years."

"Yes, I remember you saying that."

"Eddie's father—Old Man Moyer—always treated me like more of a friend than a hired hand. We spent a lot of time fishing and hunting together. Don't think he'd take kindly to his son's activities of late. And I know his heart would be broken if he realized we'd had a falling out."

"A falling out?" I queried.

"Yes." He paused and then sighed. "It's going to sound ridiculous, I know, but we had a little disagreement over. . .well. . .over a tree."

"Excuse me?" A tree?

"Yes. It's one of the oldest in Pennsylvania, an eastern hemlock."

"Our state tree?" I queried.

"Yes. It sits in the middle of the property," Roever explained. "I've been tending to it since I started working for the Moyer family. Watched its bark change in color over the years. Pruned it back. Swept up its cones. That tree and I have had a lot of good years together."

"And. . . ?"

"Eddie has his heart set on cutting it down to make room for. . ." Roever paused. "I'm so sorry. I shouldn't be telling you this. I'm completely out of line, and I hope you'll forgive me."

Hmm. Maybe he didn't have Sasha after all. If the man couldn't gossip without feeling guilty, I somehow doubted he could steal jewels from dead people and pawn them for profit.

Unless he happened to be acting right now.

I slipped my sleuthing antennae a bit higher to see if I could get better reception. "The Bible says we all sin and fall short of the glory of God, Mr. Roever. So don't feel too bad."

"Well, thank you for that, Mrs. Peterson. Makes me feel better."

Okay. Either his acting skills were phenomenal or my discernment skills were sliding down a slippery slope.

"What will you do with your time now that you're

not working at the cemetery?"

"Go fishing. Travel. Putter around in my garden. I've been so busy that I've hardly taken care of my own patch of ground." He went into a lengthy description of the weeds that had grown up in his flower beds and how he planned to deal with them. Then he shifted into a story about the kinds of flowers he hoped to plant over the next few weeks.

The most remarkable idea came to me. Maybe, if Jim Roever turned out *not* to be a murderer, I could invite him to speak to our ladies' Bible study group. With a thumb as green as his, Diedre was sure to think he hung the moon. In spite of the fact that he wasn't Irish. On the other hand, if Jim Roever *did* turn out to be a murderer, they might just hang *me*.

13

INCH BY INCH, ROW BY ROW

I pulled into the parking lot of Moyer's at eleven on Wednesday morning and found it full of cars. Maggie was right. There were a lot of funerals in Clark County. How come I'd never noticed before? Because most of them hadn't impacted me personally, perhaps?

Entering through the double doors, I stepped inside the spacious foyer hoping to find Louise McGillicuddy. I needed to ask her about Sasha. Unfortunately, she wasn't seated at the front desk today. Instead, a perfectly made-up woman with stylish auburn hair and slick red nails greeted me.

"Welcome to Moyer's." She flashed a welcoming smile. "Can I help you?"

My supersleuthing skills kicked in, and I noted her name tag: GLORIA MOYER. Must be Eddie's new wife. *What role do you play in this, Gloria? Stealing jewels from the deceased, perhaps?* I glanced down at her left hand, noticing a hefty diamond ring. Granted, it was on her ring finger. Still, it could've been stolen.

"I had hoped to talk with Ms. McGillicuddy."

"Could you wait a moment? I'll go get her."

She disappeared down the hallway, and I began to inch my way through the foyer—in search of what, I couldn't be sure. A photograph on the wall caught my attention. I stared in silence at what must be a Moyer family photo. Eddie—a younger version of himself—stood alongside a tall man with similar attributes. Likely his father. And the man off to Eddie's right must be a brother. Another man stood off to the side—in the distance, really. Was that. . .Jim Roever? Yes, it appeared to be the kindly caretaker. Only he wasn't dressed like a caretaker in this picture, was he? No, he fit right in with the other fellows.

A noise at the front door caught my attention. I turned, stunned, as my gaze landed on Sergeant O'Henry. All my suspicions were confirmed with just one look into his eyes. Fiona Kelly had not died of natural causes.

"Annie, what are you doing here?" The crease between his brows deepened.

"Same as you."

He gave me the oddest look, and for a second I half expected him to say he'd come to attend the funeral that was taking place inside the chapel. Or to purchase a prearranged funeral plan for himself. But I knew better. He'd come because Fiona Kelly had been murdered. Of that I was suddenly quite sure.

Gloria returned with Louise at her side. The second Louise laid eyes on Sergeant O'Henry, she paled.

"Officer, can I help you?" Gloria gave O'Henry a forced smile, but I could see her eyelashes fluttering double time, a sure sign of nerves. *What are you hiding, Gloria?*

"Yes, I need to speak with Mr. Moyer in his office." O'Henry directed his next words at Louise. "And if it's possible, I'd like Ms. McGillicuddy to join us."

Gloria's demeanor did not change as she spoke. "Eddie's wrapping up a service in the chapel but will be out in a few minutes. Why don't you two go ahead and wait in his office?"

As they disappeared into the inner sanctum, Gloria turned back to me. I took note of the trembling in her hands. "I'm so sorry, Mrs. Peterson. I guess you'll have to come back another time. That is, unless you're willing to wait to speak with Louise."

"I'll wait. I don't mind a bit." I took a seat in one of the wingback chairs. After some time, I heard music coming from inside the chapel. The doors opened, signaling the end of the funeral service. People swarmed toward me, many of them in tears.

I watched Gloria closely as Eddie entered the hallway. Saw her slip over to him and whisper something in his ear. Saw his brow wrinkle. Took note of the flushed cheeks.

Moyer gave his new bride a quick kiss then passed by me without so much as a glance and entered his office.

Now what? I wanted to follow along behind him, wanted to be privy to their conversation. Instead, I was stuck. . .here.

As my nerves kicked in, I rose from my seat and began to pace the front hallway. I noticed Gloria looking my way, so I offered a relaxed smile. An idea occurred to me. Perhaps I could sit in on the conversation without anyone noticing.

I slipped into the ladies' room and climbed atop the toilet in the first stall. It was one of those lidless ones, so I had to straddle the crazy thing to keep from falling in, but from here I could almost hear every word coming through the vent in the wall. . .the vent that—just as I'd suspected—led directly into Moyer's office. And if I squinted, yes, I could almost see the people inside. At least the shapes of the people.

I made out O'Henry's voice, though his words were a bit muffled. "Mr. Moyer, I've got some bad news." I strained to hear, though the words came in snatches: "Preliminary. . .autopsy. . .Fiona Kelly. . .not natural causes."

I knew it! I wanted to shout but stopped myself. So my discernment *wasn't* slipping.

On the other hand, *I* might be, if I didn't watch myself. I pressed my hands against the wall, trying to maintain my balance as I attempted to hear more.

"W–what do you mean?" Eddie sounded dumbfounded. Was he truly stunned or playing a part? I tried to get a look at his face but couldn't. Not from this angle, anyway.

"Fiona Kelly. . .poisoned," I made out.

O'Henry drew nearer to the vent, and I pulled back, praying he couldn't see—or hear—me from the other side.

"Poisoned?" I heard the disbelief in Eddie's voice.

With O'Henry standing close, I now heard every word. "The official cause of death is acute pesticide poisoning."

"Pesticide?" I whispered the word, astounded.

"Victims of pesticide poisoning often seem as if they'd died of natural causes," O'Henry explained. "But in this case the autopsy report tells the real story. Erosion of the airways and esophagus. A pungent odor in the stomach, contents an unusual color. There's no doubt she died of pesticide poisoning. The only question is, was it accidental or intentional?"

"W—what do you mean?" Eddie sounded surprised enough, but was he? "Are you saying that someone here at Moyer's poisoned her intentionally?"

"I'm not saying anything of the kind, Mr. Moyer. Please stay calm."

I recognized the sound in O'Henry's voice, had heard it many times. He was digging. Tilling the soil.

"Fiona Kelly was a florist," O'Henry explained. "And a gardener. I'm sure she and Ms. Preston used all sorts of pesticides. I plan to go by her shop when I leave here to have a look-see. And we'll check out her house, too."

"That's the only thing that makes sense." Moyer sounded relieved. I didn't blame him. Still, I wasn't sure we could let him off the hook just yet.

"Could be any number of things," O'Henry said. "But I would like to talk with you about what happened after she arrived. I need to know the order of events from the moment she first complained of not feeling well."

"Of course."

"Do you remember Fiona acting strangely?" O'-Henry asked.

"Not at first." This time it was Louise who spoke. "She was acting perfectly normal when she arrived."

"She made the delivery then came into my office to chat," Moyer explained. "We hadn't seen each other in ages and had a lot of catching up to do. I guess she was in here about an hour or more when she first started complaining of not feeling well. She started feeling dizzy and said she had a headache. Then she complained of chest pain. I didn't know what to think."

"Those symptoms would be consistent with pesticide poisoning. What else?"

"She started making a gasping noise." Moyer cleared his throat. "All I can say is that it scared me to death. I thought for a minute there she was choking. She. . .she . . .collapsed. I was sure she'd had a heart attack or some sort of seizure, so I called for Louise."

"I came right away," Louise explained. "I'm trained in CPR, so I started it at once."

"And I called 911," Moyer said. "They were here within fifteen minutes. All that time Louise worked on her. She never stopped trying to get a heartbeat."

Wow. So Louise, if she could be believed, had done her best to save Fiona's life. That put a whole new spin on things. I leaned closer, not wanting to miss a word.

"I knew she was gone." Louise sighed. "It broke my heart. I kept thinking I'd get a pulse. . .but I never did."

"You mentioned choking." This time it was O'Henry's voice. "Was she eating something?"

I startled at Moyer's response. "Brownies."

I felt my heart leap into my throat and nearly lost my balance on the toilet.

"Brownies?" O'Henry, Louise, and I spoke the word at exactly the same time.

"I offered her one when she first came into my office. She said she'd skipped lunch that day and was plenty hungry. By the time she collapsed, she'd had at least two. Maybe three. I wasn't really paying that much attention. Just remember thinking she must have really liked them."

"Well, that answers my next question," the officer continued. "The coroner found several ounces of some sort of chocolate product in her stomach and traces of it on her teeth. I suppose it's possible she had the pesticide on her hands when she arrived then reached to grab the brownies, thereby ingesting it. Or. . ."

Oh, my goodness. The revelation hit hard and fast. The plate of brownies on Moyer's desk. . . Had Louise McGillicuddy added an extra ingredient to that particular batch. . .one meant to put an end to the life of the man who had jilted her? Had her scheme gone awry when the wrong person took the first bite? My mind reeled at the possibility. Moyer had said it himself—he hadn't eaten any of the brownies. His wife wouldn't let him. That diet had saved his life. If, in fact, the brownies had carried the poison. We hadn't yet established that.

Slow down, Annie. I drew in a deep breath and tried to still my heart, which had shifted into overdrive.

Moyer sounded dumbfounded as he posed his next question. "Do you think the brownies could have been. . .?"

O'Henry's words sounded strained. "I suppose it's a possibility. Not sure how the baking process would affect the chemical makeup of the pesticide. I'm assuming the brownies are long gone by now, right?"

"I tossed them a couple of days later," Moyer said. "I, um, didn't want Louise to see that I hadn't eaten them."

"Why would I care?" The irritation in Louise's voice stunned me.

"Well, I knew you baked them specially for me, as always." Was that softness in Moyer's voice? Sensitivity?

"You baked the brownies, Ms. McGillicuddy?" O'Henry's tone changed immediately.

Her voice trembled as she responded. "I—I did not!"

"Of course you did." Moyer's volume intensified. "You baked them. You're the only one who's ever baked brownies and put them on my desk."

"N–no!" I heard her force back a sob. "Officer, you have to believe me. I haven't baked brownies since the day Eddie, er, Mr. Moyer got married. I promise."

"But there were brownies on my desk the day Fiona died." I squinted to see Moyer's expression through the holes in the vent. Tight. Angry. "If you didn't put them there, who did?"

Louise shook her head. "I don't have a clue, but I can assure you, it wasn't me. My brownie-baking days are behind me now."

"So you're saying you never even saw the brownies?" O'Henry queried.

"Never baked them. Never saw them. Never touched them."

I wanted to jump through the vent to tell O'Henry that *I'd* seen them—the day after Fiona's death. A chill came over me as I realized I'd almost reached out and grabbed one of those poisonous delights. What had stopped me again? Oh yes. . .my dimpled thighs. They'd finally come in handy.

Resisting the temptation to eat a brownie had saved my life. I could've met my Maker at Moyer's Funeral Home that fateful Thursday. Instead, the Lord had spared me.

"I think you're barking up the wrong tree," Louise added. "You need to be questioning Jim Roever."

"Roever?" Through the vent I saw O'Henry reach for his pad and scribble down the name.

"Yes, Roever." Moyer snapped his fingers. "That makes perfect sense. He's been plenty mad at me for weeks. I think he knew I was going to let him go. Maybe he. . ."

Wow. Jim Roever. He had access. He had motive. He had pesticides. He surely knew Louise's patterns . . .knew she'd baked brownies every Wednesday. He'd probably eaten quite a few of them over the years. Had the old caretaker set out to murder Eddie Moyer out of revenge over. . .a tree? Had he baked a poisonous batch of brownies and placed them on Moyer's desk when no one was looking, hoping his boss would take the bait?

Now I could hear Louise crying. Her words were muffled. "Fiona. . .full of life. . .everything to live for."

I heard the bathroom door swing open, and I scrambled down from the toilet and turned to sit on it as a voice rang out. "Mrs. Peterson?"

Oh dear. Gloria.

"Are you all right? You've been in here so long. . .I was starting to get worried."

"Oh, I, um. . ." I spoke from inside the stall. "I'm not feeling well."

That wasn't a lie. No sir. I *wasn't* feeling well.

In fact, I wasn't sure when I'd ever felt worse.

14

FRESH AS A DAISY

As soon as I left the funeral home, I telephoned Sheila and gave her the news. She responded with a gasp. "Oh, Annie, we were right."

Silence took over for a few seconds as we contemplated the fact that we'd both been tuned in to the same discernment frequency from the get-go.

"It's creepy, isn't it?" she asked at last.

"Yes, but I must admit, I'm a little relieved. Sad for Fiona but relieved in some strange way."

"Me, too. It's like I've been waiting for the other ax to fall."

"Yes. I've been the same way."

"Do you still feel up to going to church?" she asked.

"Yes, but I need to stop off at the house and let Copper out. He's a little lonely these days without Sasha there. Though. . ." I couldn't help but smile. "Warren has suddenly taken an interest in the little guy."

"No way."

"Yeah. On Saturday he taught him to sit and roll over, and yesterday he learned to beg. It's the cutest thing." I went off on a tangent about the dog but had to stop after a few seconds because thinking of Copper, as always, made me miss Sasha all the more. After a moment of silent contemplation, I asked Sheila a question that had been bothering me. "Do you think it's okay to pray for a dog?"

"You want another dog?"

"No, I mean I'm praying for Sasha. . .every day. Praying that she's safe. Praying that whoever has her is taking good care of her. And praying that they return her to us as soon as possible."

"Ah. I see."

"I just wonder if, with all the chaos and strife in the world, I'm taking up too much of the Lord's time on a canine."

"Annie, God cares as much about Sasha as you do. And He cares even more about *you* than He does about her. So I would imagine that anything affecting you is important enough to pray about."

"Thanks." I released a sigh, feeling the weight lift a little. "Are you headed up to the church?"

"Soon. I'm changing into my new outfit. Wait till you see."

Good grief. The woman must have opened a new charge card just for gardening clothes alone.

"You want to hear something funny?" she asked. "I really like digging in the dirt. And I'm actually excited about planting the flowers today."

"Really?" I contemplated her words then added, "Funny you should say that. I'm enjoying it myself."

"Oh, speaking of flowers. . ." She paused. "Maggie closed up the shop early today. Odd, huh?"

"Very." I pondered that a moment. Seemed like Maggie had been MIA a lot lately. *Hmm.*

We ended our call, and I made my way back to Clarksborough, stopping off at my house to let the dog out. Doing so reminded me that, in all the pandemonium at the funeral home, I'd forgotten to ask

Louise about Sasha. I'd have to do that next time.

Before leaving, I reached down to box Copper's ears. He looked up at me with that pitiful "When is my wife coming home?" look.

"I'll keep praying," I promised. "And you might want to do the same."

Not that the dog could pray—to my knowledge—but his begging skills were pretty good.

I offered him a treat then headed off to the church. When I pulled up in front of the courtyard area, I could hardly believe my eyes. Several buckets of red, yellow, and orange gerbera daisies caught my eye. They caught the sunlight, putting off a reflective shimmer. "Wow! They're gorgeous."

Suddenly I could hardly wait to get my hands in the dirt. I parked the car and joined the others, curious as to Sheila's whereabouts. Her car pulled in several minutes later and she emerged wearing a pair of jeans, a T-shirt, and a baseball cap.

Baseball cap?

As she made her way toward us, I read the words on the front of her T-shirt: WHEN YOU THROW DIRT, YOU LOSE GROUND. *Fascinating.* My gaze shifted to the cap, which bore a single word: DIGGER.

"Good grief."

Looking at Sheila's cap got me to thinking about Jim Roever. Thinking about Jim Roever reminded me of today's news about the cause of Fiona Kelly's death. Reflecting on Fiona caused me to wonder why Maggie Preston had put the CLOSED sign on the shop early today. Wondering about the sign on the flower shop door reminded me that I was here not to think but to work. Thinking about work shifted my thoughts to my clients. Pondering my clients somehow reminded me that Candy and I still had a lot of work to do before her wedding day. And thinking of the wedding somehow brought me back around to the courtyard in front of me.

Goodness. I really needed to do something about this ADD.

I looked up as I heard Diedre's happy-go-lucky voice. "Ladies, are we ready to get to work?" She looked as if she might burst from excitement.

We gathered round, and she gave us instructions on the planting process. Some of the women were handed packets of seeds; others were given what Diedre referred to as germinated seeds, and Sheila and I ended up with the buckets of daisies.

Diedre drew near our section of the garden and gave us some instructions. "Start by digging holes for your plants," she instructed. "You don't want to go any deeper than they are in the containers."

"How far apart?" Sheila knelt down on the ground with a hand shovel, ready to get to work.

"About a foot or so," Diedre explained. "But before you do your planting, add a bit of fertilizer to the hole you've dug. Then pull the daisy plant from the container, dirt and all, and drop it down into the hole."

Sheila went to work at once, digging the first hole. Wearing her ergonomically designed gloves, of course. This time around, she seemed at home on her knees, something that struck me as rather odd until I realized she'd been at home on her knees for years. Praying, not gardening. But it was all seed planting, right?

All the while, Diedre kept a watchful eye on us, helping out folks as they needed her assistance. She paused to encourage some of the women who looked as if they'd rather be at the mall.

"I always say that gardening is a matter of your enthusiasm holding up until your back gets used to it." Diedre giggled. "So stay enthused, women. Your bodies will eventually catch up."

As I stretched my aching arms and back, I prayed she was right. Though I'd grown to enjoy gardening, I wasn't so sure it was enjoying me.

After we wrapped up in the courtyard, we all stood back and admired our handiwork.

"Wow. That's quite a transformation," Sheila observed.

"Breathtaking," I whispered.

"It's pretty amazing how a fresh planting can change your whole outlook on life," Evelyn explained. "Adding all this color to the courtyard gives the whole building a face-lift."

I had to agree. Something about all the color simply made my head swim. And knowing we'd put something in the soil that would continue to grow and blossom just gave me. . .hope.

After a few more oohs and aahs, we went inside for more of Janetta's amazing vegetable-themed goodies. Tonight's menu included three varieties of homemade hummus and pita bread, along with grilled vegetable kabobs. The woman was becoming a virtual Proverbs 31 woman in front of our very eyes. I couldn't help but think that she'd one day make a fine wife for some great fella.

At Evelyn's urging, we had invited our families to join us for dinner. Devin turned up his nose at the hummus at first but later admitted that he actually enjoyed it. Warren was partial to the grilled vegetables, commenting on Janetta's skills and thanking her for her hard work. She turned several shades of red then disappeared into the kitchen to tidy things up.

At seven o'clock, we sent the menfolk to their classroom and the kids to their various groups, and we settled in for what I knew would turn out to be another great teaching.

Evelyn opened in prayer then thanked us all for our hard work in the garden. She reached for her Bible and got down to business.

"Diedre felt I should share this particular lesson with you, and I can hardly wait. I can't tell you how excited I am about the planting we've done today. There's just something about transplanting flowers into the soil that gets me charged up."

I had to admit, it was starting to get me excited, too. And I could see enthusiasm written all over Sheila. Something about this "Consider a Field" project was getting to us.

"Last week we tilled our hearts," Evelyn reminded us. "Softened the soil. Asked God to heal our hurts and our wounds. The reason it's so important to be healed from the past is because there's so much work to be done. . .today. I think the Proverbs 31 woman understood this. The woman epitomized hard work. Why, she worked from sunup till sundown."

With the aches and pains settling in, I felt her pain.

"God wants us to reach this world for Him. We're

called to go into all the world and preach the gospel." Evelyn shook her head. "I never really understood that verse as a child. Couldn't figure out how I was supposed to go into all the world when I couldn't even travel by myself. But I understand it now. My 'world' is the area where I live. I'm supposed to bloom where I'm planted. Do what I can *where* I can, *when* I can, and *how* I can to reach others with the love of Christ.

"One of my favorite verses is Matthew 13:24, the second half." Evelyn glanced down at her Bible as she read, " 'The kingdom of heaven is like a man who sowed good seed in his field.' " She looked up at us with a smile. "We're always talking about how we want to see God's kingdom come and His will be done. Isn't it interesting that the Lord uses this analogy of good seeds?"

I wasn't completely sure where she was going with this but paid careful attention.

Evelyn looked at her notes then gazed at us with excitement flashing in her eyes. "I like to think of it like this: All the flowers of all the tomorrows are in the seeds of today. In other words, all the people who will come into the kingdom tomorrow come as a result of the seeds we plant today. If I don't plant good seeds— and by that I mean sharing my testimony; living a godly life; caring for those in need; reaching out to the poor, the homeless, the downtrodden; treating others as I want to be treated—then I won't see any flowers. And I'm called to do all that right here, where God has planted me."

She gave us a sly smile. "That's not to say I'm limited to Clarksborough, PA, mind you. I'm trying to talk that sweet hubby of mine into taking me on a missions trip to Central America. If and when that time comes, I plan to take several of you with me."

Wow. If I made it through this season of wedding planning, I'd love to join them. What would Warren think? Would he like to travel to foreign shores?

Evelyn held up a packet of seeds with the words GERBERA DAISIES imprinted on the front. It was wrapped with a pink satin ribbon. "I want you to look at this," she explained. "Inside this packet is the potential for a garden as beautiful as the one we planted today. But if I don't plant these seeds, it's just potential. Nothing actually comes of it."

Okay, I was starting to get it now.

Evelyn nodded in Diedre's direction. Diedre stood and reached under her table, pulling out a basket filled with seed packets.

"Diedre and I thought it would be a good idea to give each of you a packet of seeds," Evelyn explained. "We want you to think about the people God has placed in your lives, the ones you see on a daily basis and the ones you only see once in a while. Think of them as daisies. If you reach out to others with the love of Christ, you are a worker in the vineyard. You're planting seeds. And the more you plant, the larger the garden you receive. Before you know it, the world is filled with color and fragrance. We become an aroma of praise to God."

I paused to think about her words. Who had God placed in my life that I could reach out to with His love? My family, sure. And my friends. But who else?

"Next week we're going to talk about the

importance of watering and fertilization. We're also going to talk about the need for adequate sunlight." Diedre joined Evelyn at the front of the room. "These are critical ingredients to a plant's growth. In the meantime, let's divide up into small groups again and spend some time putting together lists of names of the people we can reach out to."

As I rose from my seat, I thought about that packet of daisy seeds and all of the untapped potential inside. With God's help, I would become a seed planter.

15

WALLFLOWER

The following morning I awoke thinking of daisies. During my quiet time, after I read through the thirt-first chapter of Proverbs one more time, I asked the Lord to show me the people He'd placed in my life, the ones I needed to spend time sharing His love with. Two people came to mind at once. . .after my friends and family members, of course. Maggie Preston and Roger Kratz.

Maggie had been on my mind a lot lately. Something about her demeanor over the past couple of weeks had left me feeling uneasy. Maybe, like Roger, she just needed a friend. We hadn't seen her much in church of late. I sensed she would do well to be surrounded by friends. Perhaps I could plant a few seeds and she'd blossom over time.

I also found myself thinking about—and praying for—Roger Kratz. Yeah, he was a testy old fellow, but he was also alone. . .with no wife to tend to his needs. He could probably use a good friend right about now. I made up my mind to visit with him. Maybe I'd even take him some baked goods. He was partial to that cinnamon-swirl coffee cake.

At a quarter till eight, Warren stuck his head in the office door and gave me a smile. "Editing?"

"Yes, but not for long. I have some things to take care of."

"Things?" He paused a moment then gave me a

pensive look. "I read the paper, Annie. Be careful."

"I will. I promise."

"Mm-hmm." He pursed his lips then glanced at the clock. "Gotta run. Call me if you need anything. I'm only working a half day today, remember?"

"Oh, that's right." I'd almost forgotten that the bank was getting a new AC system today.

Warren gave me a wink that melted my heart. "I love you, Annie."

I rose to kiss him good-bye then whispered, "I love you, too," in his ear. My heart swelled with joy as his cheeks flushed pink. The man still made my heart flutter, even after all these years.

Around ten o'clock I wrapped up my work and headed over to Flowers by Fiona to visit with Maggie Preston. I breathed a sigh of relief when I saw the OPEN sign on the door. I entered the store but found it empty. Odd.

"Maggie?" I called out, hoping she'd emerge from the back room.

She came out with a bundle of roses in her hand and a forced smile on her face. "Hey, Annie. Good to see you."

Her words might be positive and upbeat, but the red-rimmed eyes contradicted them in every conceivable way. *What's going on with you, Maggie? Are you struggling with Fiona's death, or is there more, perhaps?*

"I saw the paper." She sighed, and I realized why she probably looked so down today. This morning's *Clark County Gazette* had probably startled most of Clarksborough's residents with its LOCAL FLORIST POISONED headline. "It was one thing to suspect it but another to have it confirmed."

"I know."

"O'Henry's been here three times," she said. "Looking through all our cabinets. Going through Fiona's house with a fine-tooth comb. I still get the feeling that he thinks I plotted this. If only he knew. . ." She shook her head and brushed away a loose tear. "I loved Fiona. She took me under her wing and cared for me through thick and thin. She was the only one I ever shared all my secrets with." Her eyes flashed with anger. "But they're not the kind of secrets O'Henry has in mind. I didn't have anything to do with what happened to Fiona."

"I think he's just digging for answers," I explained. "It's part of the process."

"Still. . ." She shrugged. "I hate being part of that process. Makes me feel. . .I don't know. . .makes me feel guilty when I know I didn't do anything. Does that make sense?"

"Of course." My conscience began to bother me at once. After all, I'd stopped by to question her, just as O'Henry had done. I turned to face her with what I hoped came across as a compassionate look on my face.

"I hate to bother you." I made my apologies up front. "But I've been intrigued by a comment you made the other day. You insinuated that Fiona knew something about Eddie Moyer. Thought he was up to something."

"Ah."

"Would you be willing to talk about it now that we know the truth of Fiona's death?"

I hoped she'd come out and say it. . .say that Fiona had suspected Eddie of pawning the jewels of the deceased. Instead, Maggie went a completely different direction.

"I really don't want to betray a confidence," she whispered.

"I'm not asking you to do that. But I do want you to know that the story of what happened to Fiona is unraveling, and I want to do what I can to help. So anything you can tell me would help. And who knows . . .you might have the very clue that leads me to the person responsible for Fiona's death."

"I can't imagine this as any kind of a clue," she said. "I just know. . ." She looked around to make sure that no one had entered the shop. "I just know that Louise McGillicuddy is a good woman. We've become friends over the years. And I know that she. . ." Maggie's voice trailed off, and I reached to touch her arm.

"She what?"

"She's been in love with Eddie for as many years as I've known her," Maggie explained. "She would do anything for him."

"Anything?" *Like pawn jewels, for instance?*

"Until a few months ago, when he met Gloria." Maggie groaned. "This is what gets me. Gloria is a recent widow. Her husband only died about ten months ago. She met Eddie while planning her husband's funeral. They got married five months later." Maggie shook her head, and a look of anger flashed in her eyes. "Can you believe that? I mean, Louise cared for Eddie for fifteen years. And she thought. . ."

"Thought he loved her, too?" I offered.

"Yes." Maggie sighed. "In many ways, they were already like husband and wife. Counted on each other for everything."

I thought at once of the brownies Louise had baked for Eddie. Must've been quite a love offering. Until that last batch, anyway.

Stop it, Annie. You don't even know if she baked those brownies.

Maggie carried on, clearly oblivious to my thoughts. "Gloria started showing up more and more, and Eddie's attentions shifted. Gloria's a pretty woman and a wealthy one, too. That's one thing I know about Eddie Moyer. He's a man who likes nice things." She paused then asked a question. "Have you seen his new vacation home out on the lake? It's amazing."

"No, I haven't," I admitted, "but I'd like to."

"He and Gloria also have a great home in Wallop— an old farmhouse, fully renovated. I can tell you where he lives, if you're interested." Maggie's eyes flashed with anger. "He's ordered flowers for Gloria nearly a dozen times over the past several months and had them delivered there."

"Newlywed stuff." I sighed. How long had it been since Warren had sent me flowers? Three years? Four?

"Would you believe he wanted Fiona to take care of the flowers for his wedding? She flat-out refused. Said she wouldn't break Louise's heart by doing such a thing." Maggie looked over at me with a shrug. "Fiona and Louise were always good friends."

"I had no idea."

"Well, they were both plenty busy, so they weren't friends in the same sense that, say, you and Sheila are.

But they'd known each other for years. We all had."

"And you think Louise's heart was broken when Eddie married?"

"Of course. The evening of his wedding, I offered to take her out to dinner and a movie. She didn't want to go—at first. But I eventually talked her into it."

"Can I ask you a question?"

"Sure."

"The day Fiona passed away. You were supposed to make the delivery to Moyer's."

Maggie's gaze shifted down. "Y–yes."

"And she went in your place."

"She did."

"You were in Philly."

"Yes." She shook her head. "I know it sounds strange that I'd happen to be gone on that very day," she explained. "But you'll have to trust me on this one, Annie. I'll tell you what I was doing in Philly. . .soon. But not yet."

Hmm. I wanted to trust her. But the more I found out about her ties to the folks at Moyer's, the more I wondered if she could be trusted. Had she and Louise conspired to take Eddie's life only to end up taking Fiona's instead?

A cold chill enveloped me as those seeds of suspicion took root. Perhaps in time they would begin to grow. In the meantime, I needed to pay Roger Kratz a little visit. Perhaps I could talk Warren into coming along with me. He had the afternoon off, after all. I telephoned him, explained the situation, and he readily agreed. We set off for Wallop minutes later.

As we pulled into town, I decided to stop off at a

grocery store and pick up a coffee cake. I also decided to stop off at PA Perk for a bag of coffee, explaining the significance to Warren. Perhaps Roger would welcome us into his home if we came bearing gifts.

At 1:35 I gave Roger a call. He answered on the third ring, and though he seemed surprised to hear we wanted to come by for a visit, he welcomed us. I whispered a prayer of thanks, knowing the Lord had opened this door. Now for a little seed planting.

As I pulled the car up in front of his house, I paused for a moment to examine his lawn. *Hmm.*

"Wow. Kind of a mess," Warren commented.

"Sure is." His garden was completely overgrown with weeds, and the grass could have used a good mowing. In all, the place looked pretty run-down, as if the owner had simply given up. Maybe, in some strange way, all of this chaos brought comfort to Roger Kratz.

My thoughts shifted to Jim Roever. I pondered how the two men were alike and how they were different. Perhaps I should introduce them to each other. Maybe Jim's great gardening skills would rub off on Roger, and maybe Roger's sarcastic sense of humor would rub off on Jim.

After a few seconds, a rap on my window startled me. I eased the glass down a few inches as Roger's face came into view.

"Are you two coming in or not?" he asked.

"Oh. . ." I turned off the car and reached for the coffee and cake. "We're coming."

We tagged along behind him as he led the way to the house. Entering through the front door, I found myself in a narrow entryway that emptied into a living room. The area was cluttered with far more than the usual furnishings. I'd never seen so many newspapers, books, dishes, and laundry.

Poor guy. Looked like he really needed someone to sweep in and help him get this place organized.

As if reading my thoughts, Roger offered an apology. "Betty would've had my head for this." He pointed to the room. "She was the cleanest person I ever knew. Maybe that's why I'm at such a loss. She always did everything around here. Me. . ." He sighed. "It's taken me all these months just to figure out where things are."

"I'm so sorry, Mr. Kratz." Warren spoke up, compassion lacing his words.

"Call me Roger. I think we're past the formalities now." He glanced down at the cake in my hands. "Is that for me?"

"It is. But I'd like to have a piece, if you don't mind."

Not that my thighs needed it, but who was keeping track?

"I'll just take it to the kitchen." He snagged the cake and headed down a long hallway just beyond the living room. Though he didn't offer an invite, I followed him anyway, and Warren tagged along on my heels. I could hardly believe my eyes when we landed in the tiny kitchen. I'd seen dishes stack up at my house on occasion, but never like this. My heart went out to the poor man. Maybe I should arrange for the W.O.W. ladies to spend a Saturday afternoon whipping his house into shape. On the other hand, he might be offended at the suggestion.

As he put the cake on the counter, I noticed a plate of cookies nearby. Homemade, no less. "Did you make those?" I queried.

He shrugged. "Yeah. I enjoy baking. Cakes, cookies, brownies, pies. . .all sorts of things."

He bakes brownies? Hmm. Very interesting.

Roger drew in a deep breath as he reached for a knife to slice the cake. "Might sound crazy, but it makes me feel closer to Betty. She used to bake all the time. I didn't realize I'd been paying attention, but I must've been, because I've been able to replicate most of her recipes." He chuckled. "Now if only I could figure out where she kept the password for our online checking account, I'd be in great shape. Well, that and the spare keys to the car." The edges of his lips turned up in a smile.

As I watched the poor fellow search for clean plates, I had to wonder if he would ever be in great shape again. How could you move forward after losing a spouse, particularly one you'd been married to for forty-three years? My heart twisted at the very idea. I reached over to squeeze Warren's hand.

"I'm not sure how I would function without Annie," Warren admitted.

"And vice versa," I whispered.

Roger put the coffee on to brew, and I turned my attention, once again, to his house. Something about being here made me uncomfortable. In spite of the fact that I'd come to plant seeds, to share the love of the Lord, I couldn't get past the nagging feeling that something about Roger just felt wrong.

From the backyard, something caught my attention. A barking dog. My heart leaped as I heard it. Sounded like a small dog. . .kind of like. . .

"Hang on a second," Roger said. "Gotta take care of Butch."

"Butch?" Warren chuckled. "Must be a tough one."

"Oh yeah." Roger opened the back door and a tiny black Pomeranian entered, one in serious need of grooming. The little fuzzy pup began to jump up and down, and without even asking, I reached to snatch him into my arms.

"He's adorable, Roger." I let the pup nuzzle his cold little nose against my cheek. Oh, how I missed Sasha! Holding this little darling only made it worse.

"Butch was Betty's dog," Roger said. "His real name is Beau, but I thought that was too girly, so I always called him Butch just to irritate her." He sighed. "I never used to like the little mongrel, to be quite honest." Roger released a sigh. "But since she's been gone, I've. . . ."

"Gotten attached?" Warren asked.

"Yes." He shrugged. "But don't spread that around. Don't want people to think I'm a sissy."

Right away, his eyes filled with tears. I deliberately shifted my gaze to let him off the hook. Rubbing the little dog behind the ears served as a nice distraction but also made my heart ache for Sasha.

With coffee cups filled and slices of coffee cake on freshly washed plates, we made our way over to the small dinette table. Roger explained that the old Formica table had been a wedding gift in the midsixties.

"If I had my way, life would be like this old table," he explained. "Nothing would ever change. I'd stop the clock if I could."

"But where would you stop it?" Warren asked. "I mean, what year? Sometime in the sixties?"

He shrugged. "Probably not that far back. We didn't have our kids till the early seventies. I'd like to include them in this far-fetched fantasy of mine."

"The seventies, then?" I queried. "Or the eighties?"

"I don't know." He sighed. "I know I can't really change anything. But I do wish my wife had outlived me. That's how I always thought it would be. I certainly never thought I'd have to pick out her casket or figure out what dress—or jewelry—to bury her in." Roger's jaw grew tight. "Not that I would have wanted her to go through any of that for me, either." He shook his head. "When I die, I just want someone to put me in a pine box. Or cremate me. But I do not. . ."—he began to visibly tremble—"do *not* want Moyer's Funeral Home to have anything to do with it."

The anger that gripped him alarmed me. I hadn't seen this side of him, at least not to this extent.

"I've left specific instructions with my kids." Roger seemed to hold in his breath, and the tips of his ears reddened. "They know better than to contact Moyer when I go. If I had my way, I'd put him out of business. I don't know how I'd go about it exactly, but if I had the time—or the energy—I'd think of something."

I didn't offer my thoughts on the matter, in part because I hadn't quite made up my mind about Eddie Moyer. Sure, it appeared he'd stolen the jewels and pawned them for profit, but what proof did I have, really? Just Roger's word. For all I knew, he could've made the whole thing up. The fact that he had a brooch in his possession meant nothing. How did I know he'd ever given it to Louise in the first place?

As that possibility registered, my nerves kicked in. What if Roger Kratz wasn't a nice old man? What if he'd made up the story about Moyer to get even with him for overcharging him? What if. . . I shuddered at this very thought. What if Roger really meant it when he said he'd do *anything* to put Moyer out of business?

What if *anything*. . .included murder?

16

I'M A LONELY LITTLE PETUNIA

The morning after we visited Roger Kratz, Warren surprised me by saying that he really liked the old guy, whether he was testy or not. "We should have him over for dinner sometime."

Alrighty then. We'd have him over for dinner. If I could just prove he hadn't killed Fiona. In the meantime, I had work to do. I decided that another trip to Moyer's Funeral Home was in order. Somehow in the chaos of my last trip, I'd forgotten to ask Louise about Sasha. If Jim Roever had really posted the flyers before he was fired, then surely Louise would have been on the lookout for my baby.

I arrived to find things in total chaos. The addition of O'Henry's patrol car out front further alerted me to the fact that something terrible must have happened. I stepped inside, hoping to find Louise. Instead, Eddie's wife sat at the front desk. Sobbing. I caught her in midsentence as she spoke to O'Henry.

"Like I said before, he never came home last night."

What? Eddie is missing?

O'Henry turned to glance my way then pursed his lips and turned back to Gloria. "When did you last speak to him?"

"At five forty-five, when I left the funeral home. I stopped off at the store and picked up some groceries.

These past few weeks have been so stressful. I wanted to make him a wonderful dinner. I knew he had a lot of paperwork to catch up on, but he said he'd be home by seven thirty." As she cried, her mascara ran in little black rivers under her lashes.

O'Henry scribbled a few words in his notepad. "Did you speak with him again after that?"

She shook her head and brushed away the tears, though she only managed to make a bigger mess of things. "No. I tried his office phone at seven forty-five, but he didn't answer. So I tried his cell phone. No answer there, either. I waited up all night, but he never came home."

"Mrs. Moyer, is there anything else we should know?" The tone of O'Henry's voice changed as he questioned her. "Any enemies? Anyone who might've been out to get him?"

"Well. . ." She paused and looked my way, as if suddenly realizing that I'd interrupted their conversation. "Oh, Mrs. Peterson. . . C—can I help you?"

"I, um, I'm just looking for Louise. I never had a chance to ask her about—"

"Louise," Gloria's expression hardened right away as she turned back to the officer. "That's another thing. Louise called in sick today. That never happens. Doesn't that sound suspicious to you, that she'd happen to call in sick on the same day Eddie's disappeared?"

"Are you saying you think Louise and your husband are. . .together?" O'Henry asked.

Gloria's face paled and her voice softened. "Not in the way you're implying. Eddie never had any romantic notions toward that woman, despite anything you might have heard to the contrary. I'm more concerned that she's done something to hurt him, out of spite. She's been plenty jealous of our relationship, and that's putting it nicely."

My antennae rose at once as I reflected on her words. I couldn't help but wonder what Maggie might think of this revelation. To give Gloria and O'Henry more privacy, I scooted back into the entryway, out of sight but not out of earshot.

Gloria continued to rant. "No telling what lengths Louise would go to, to hurt Eddie, now that he's married to me. I know what she said about not baking those brownies, but I can tell you for a fact, she baked them every Wednesday for years. Until I came into the picture. I still can't help but think. . ."

Her voice trailed off, and O'Henry's tone changed. I noted a bit of compassion. "Let's don't jump to conclusions, Mrs. Moyer. We have no reason to suspect foul play. Maybe your husband just decided he needed some time to himself."

"But we're practically honeymooners," she wailed. "Why would he need time away?"

Several ideas shot through my mind at once as I hid in the quiet privacy of the entryway. (1) Perhaps Moyer figured the police were on his trail about those pawned jewels and had opted for a quick getaway, or (2) maybe he really thought his life was in jeopardy and slipped away to protect himself, or (3) perhaps his relationship with Gloria wasn't all it was cracked up to be. Was he involved with Louise after all?

Hmm. Another possibility registered.

(4) Maybe Gloria, in spite of her tears and wailing,

wasn't a happy honeymooner. Maybe *she* had done something to Eddie. And maybe she'd planted those brownies, hoping to kill off husband number two. Kind of made me wonder how husband number one had died.

Several minutes later, O'Henry passed me on his way to the door. "Annie." He released a sigh as he spoke my name. "Didn't realize you were still here."

"I came to ask Louise about my dog."

"Oh yes. Sasha." He nodded. "I'd heard she'd disappeared. I'm so sorry about that."

"Thanks. I guess I can't exactly talk to Louise now." I followed the officer out to the parking lot. Instead of heading to his patrol car, he followed me to my vehicle.

"Can I ask you a couple of questions?" he asked.

"Sure." I leaned against the car and took a good look at the officer. He'd once been a Sunday school student of mine. A quarter of a century ago. How could one of my former students now be. . .balding?

O'Henry sighed. "You're a woman."

"Well, yes."

He turned to face me. "I'm just thinking you might be better at thinking this through, being female and all. And, um. . ." He hesitated a moment. "You did figure out who stole twenty-five-thousand dollars from Clark County Savings and Loan a few months ago."

"Right, right."

I could see the embarrassment in his expression as he added, "And you, um, did help figure out who kidnapped your son-in-law awhile back."

"Yes."

"Look. . ." He raked his fingers through his hair. "If Louise McGillicuddy was in love with Eddie Moyer—and I have it on good authority she was—then why would she try to kill him? If she did. I'm not saying I believe that."

"Jealousy?" I offered.

"Maybe. But I do have to wonder if maybe they've gone off someplace together."

"It's a possibility but not a strong one, to my way of thinking."

"Why do you say that?" O'Henry's blue eyes flashed with frustration.

"Simple. She's not terribly pretty and not well-to-do."

"Ouch." He laughed. "I can't believe you just said that."

"You wanted my opinion," I offered. "And that's it. Eddie Moyer is a man who likes nice things. I'm thinking Gloria fits his profile for nice-wife material, not Louise McGillicuddy. And if he cared about Louise at all, wouldn't he have shown her that in the fifteen years they worked together? Why wait till after he'd married Gloria?"

"Makes sense." After a lengthy pause, O'Henry snapped his fingers. "Maybe we're coming at this backward," he suggested. "Maybe Eddie has done something to Louise. Maybe she's the one we should be concerned about."

I sighed as I realized just how complicated this had become. If I had a lick of sense, I'd drop this investigation right now. Put it completely in O'Henry's capable hands. I needed to focus on Candy's wedding, not a funeral director and his heartbroken assistant.

Unfortunately, my mind wouldn't stop reeling. "Maybe Louise knew too much," I suggested.

"About what?"

"Well, about the pawned jewels, for one thing."

The look of shock on O'Henry's face almost made me laugh out loud. "Annie, how do you do that?"

"Do what?" I played innocent.

"I just found out about the pawned jewels this morning. How in the world did you know about them?"

"Oh, I talked to Roger Kratz. I've known for some time now."

"Roger Kratz? You actually know Roger Kratz?" He shook his head, as if he didn't quite believe me.

"Well, we're not best friends." I shrugged. "But I do know quite a few things about him. He's lonely. Mad at Moyer. Likes a good cup of coffee. Needs to mow his lawn. Seemed to get along with my husband. Bakes a mean Snickerdoodle. That alone makes him a suspect, to my way of thinking."

"Beg your pardon? Snickerdoodle?"

"Oh, it's a cookie. His wife's recipe. He likes to bake. *Brownies*, even. Don't you find that suspicious?"

"Maybe." I could almost see the wheels turning in his head. "Do you suppose there's some connection between Roger Kratz and Louise McGillicuddy?" He posed the question more as a statement.

"I've thought about that," I admitted, "but it seems far-fetched. From the moment I met Mr. Kratz, it was clear he despised everyone at Moyer's, so I have a hard time imagining him teaming up with Louise to bring harm to Eddie. . .if that's what you're getting at."

"I'm not sure what I'm getting at." O'Henry raked his fingers through his hair. "I just know that this investigation is going to age me. And until we know who killed Fiona. . .until we know for sure Eddie Moyer was the intended suspect. . .I'm not going to get much sleep."

"You should try all of this and wedding planning, too."

There must've been something in my expression that finally caused O'Henry to crack a smile. "Annie, you're incorrigible. First of all, you're *not* on the Clark County payroll. You don't need to be figuring out who killed whom. Or why."

"I know, but. . ." It wasn't like my investigation was getting in the way of his, after all. All I'd done, really, was dig up a little dirt on a few suspects.

"That's not to say I don't value your opinions or your input." O'Henry pursed his lips. "But it does get a little embarrassing when the sheriff's office ends up leaning on one of the county's residents for clues." He gave me a pensive look. "Though I'll be the first to admit I'm ready to listen if you've got any."

I offered up a shrug. "I have a head full of suspicions," I admitted. "Same as you. Nothing solid yet." I looked him in the eye. "But I'll promise you this. . ."

"Yes?"

"If I think I'm on to something—really think I'm on to something—I'll let you know. I won't put my own life at risk. Been there, done that."

"That's good to know."

As we parted ways, my mind reeled at the sudden influx of possibilities. Where was my supersleuthing notebook when I needed it? This much I knew to be true. Despite O'Henry's doubts, Fiona Kelly had not been the intended target. Someone wanted Eddie Moyer dead. And the list of suspects was growing almost as fast as the daisies in the church's courtyard.

17

The Waltz of the Flowers

The weather on Wednesday surprised us all. After a light rain the prior afternoon, the day turned out to be hot and exceptionally muggy. Quite unusual in Pennsylvania, even in late May.

Evelyn had advised us that today's visit in the garden wouldn't require as much time as usual. We were to arrive at five o'clock to discuss watering, fertilization, and sunlight. These things might not have interested me a few weeks ago, but now that I had a vested interest in the flowers, I couldn't wait to hear what Diedre had to say.

When I pulled my car into the parking lot of the church, I saw the renovated courtyard area. Even from such a distance, the vibrant colors of the daisies and marigolds nearly took my breath away. Funny how the changes we'd made gave the whole exterior of the church a face-lift. What was it called—curb appeal? Would the men notice? Had they already?

I climbed out of the car hoping that Sheila would take note of my new outfit. I'd found the T-shirt at our local supercenter. The flowers on the front weren't terribly realistic, but I loved the quote underneath: As the Garden Grows, So Does the Gardener.

Surely Sheila couldn't top this one.

Minutes later, she made her entrance in much the same way I would envision a queen arriving at a royal ball. Orin pulled their luxury sedan up to the edge of the courtyard. Nothing new there. As always, he walked around to the passenger side to open her door. As Sheila stepped out onto the pavement, I half expected to see her wearing a tiara and ball gown—something with a floral theme, of course. Instead, my jaw dropped as I took in her apparel. She wore a pair of denim overalls over a smudged white T-shirt. Her usually stylish hair was pulled up in a dingy cap. As she drew closer, I noticed circles of moist dirt on her knees.

"Hey." I flashed a smile. "Busy day?"

"Oh, Annie. . ." A wistful look came into her eyes, and for a minute I thought she might cry. "I've found myself. . .in the dirt."

"Excuse me?"

"Orin and I are planting flower gardens in our yard." Her face beamed with joy. "We started in the front with azaleas, marigolds, crocuses, and a variety of shrubs. Then we moved to the side yard. Our property is nice and big, so I figured it would be lovely to add some color."

"And Orin agreed?" I looked back at her car as he pulled away.

"Yes, he's headed back now to finish up with the garden on the east lawn before men's group tonight. He's really enjoying this."

"Wow."

"Yes." She paused to read the text on my shirt, adding, "Very cool."

"Thanks." I appreciated her compliment, but suddenly my shirt paled in comparison to the shimmer in my best friend's eyes. Diedre had rubbed off on her! Had Sheila really found herself in the dirt? If so, would I ever be able to dig her out again?

"It's so funny. . . ." She reached into the pocket of her denim overalls and came up with her ergonomically designed gloves. I gasped as I took note of their dilapidated condition. She'd actually been using them . . .to work. "I never realized how much fun it could be, working the soil. Planting. Fertilizing. . ." She glanced my way and shrugged. "And it gives me something to do now that the kids are grown and gone."

"I understand. Trust me." Many times over the past week my stomach had knotted up at the idea of both my daughters being married. Life seemed to be moving at such a rapid pace these days.

Evelyn called us to order, and we all walked to the courtyard and turned to face her. Her cheeks glowed, perhaps not as much from the afternoon sunlight as from the joy over the new garden. "How are you ladies this afternoon?"

We offered up a variety of responses, many of which made her smile.

"Today Diedre is going to start her teaching in the garden. We'll move inside when our work out here is done."

She passed the reins to Diedre, who faced us with an impish grin. "Ladies, do you see what a difference a few flowers have made?" Something about the way this beautiful Irish woman said the word *flowers* almost made my heart sing. When we nodded, she continued. "This afternoon I want to talk to you about what it means for a plant to take root and grow. We'll talk specifically about the necessary ingredients for growth: water, sunshine, and fertilizer. Are you ready to begin?"

She pointed to a row of watering cans that lined the cobblestone walkway. "These are our tools today. Use them with care."

I reached for a green plastic can, noticing that it had already been filled with water.

"Gerbera daisies need to be fertilized regularly during the warmer seasons," Diedre explained. "We've already mixed up a half-strength batch in those watering cans. I want you to saturate the soil then come back here for further instructions."

Sheila and I moseyed over to the area where we'd planted our daisies last week. "They're looking pretty good," I observed. Indeed, they nearly took my breath away. "Aw, I spoke too soon. Look at this." I found one that looked a little droopy.

"Should be better after we tend to it," Sheila assured me. She spoke with authority, and I marveled at the fact that she actually believed the little flower might actually make it. The poor little thing looked like a goner to me.

We used our watering cans to cover our area of the garden. I tended to my crop like a skilled surgeon. Not one of my little ones would die with me in charge.

Hmm. Rephrase that. I didn't really hold the power of life and death in my hands, did I? No, only the Lord could determine when something—or someone—passed away.

Suddenly I wasn't thinking about flowers anymore. Thankfully, Diedre's voice interrupted my tempestuous thoughts. "Ladies, if you're finished, join me here at the center of the walkway." We all made our way in her direction.

Diedre clutched her hands together at her chest as she addressed us. "Gardening is a way of showing that you believe in tomorrow. When you plant a garden, you're saying to everyone who watches that you truly believe tomorrow is going to come. Otherwise, why would you waste your time planting something if you didn't think it would have time to grow and blossom?"

"I never thought of it that way," I whispered to Sheila. *Gardening is a way of showing that I believe in tomorrow. Wow.*

Suddenly, looking at the colorful petals of those daisies, hope kicked in. They would continue to blossom and grow. . .and so would I. I didn't have to fear death. Even if it swept me off. . .tomorrow. After all, I knew where I'd spend eternity. Knew the Master Gardener personally. And He probably had a mansion picked out for me with a fabulous courtyard out front—one that would never need tending.

As I stood there, hope truly took root in my soul. I had no idea what tomorrow held, but I did believe it would come. For me. For Warren. For our children. For my church family. For my friendships. For my business. For my crime-solving adventures.

Diedre wrapped up the teaching with a few thoughts about the Proverbs 31 woman's internal fortitude then dismissed us to go inside for more of Janetta's amazing food. As the others headed to the fellowship hall, I made my way over to Evelyn. I'd been meaning to talk to her for days and kept forgetting.

"Evelyn, I keep forgetting to tell you something. I met this fellow. He was a caretaker at Moyer's Cemetery."

"Oh?"

"Yes, his name's Jim Roever. He does the most incredible landscaping. He's no longer working at the cemetery and is a little lonely. But with his years in the business—thirty-five years of working in the flower gardens—I truly think we could help him out by inviting him to come. And he'd be helping us, too. I'm sure he'd be thrilled to talk with us about his experience."

"Is he a believer?" Evelyn asked.

"Hmm. I haven't been able to figure that out yet," I acknowledged, "but he's a great guy. Kind of a grandfatherly figure. And I love the way he dresses. He's always wearing. . ." I looked up as Sheila passed by, realizing the truth of it. "Well, he always dresses like *that*."

Evelyn looked over at Sheila and chuckled. "I'm so glad she's enjoying this. I don't know when I've ever seen anyone have so much fun."

"Me, either."

Evelyn's expression grew more serious. "I'll pray about this caretaker fellow. You do the same. If you think he'd be a good fit for our group, I'd love to have him."

"Awesome!"

We made our way inside for snacks. My stomach rumbled at the prospect of what Janetta might've made.

"Oh, wow. Look at that." I pointed to the tables. Someone—probably Evelyn or Diedre—had done a bit of decorating. Each table had its own beautiful centerpiece. They'd used watering cans filled with silk flowers for some of them. A few of the tables had the cutest centerpieces of all: tiny gardening tools all wrapped up in ribbons and bows. Talk about clever.

Not that I cared much about clever right now. No, as my stomach grumbled, I realized that I'd forgotten to eat lunch today. I secretly hoped that Janetta had come up with something spectacular for tonight's meal.

Just then, she came out of the kitchen carrying a large salad bowl. As she placed it on the serving table, I looked inside and was perplexed to find that the lettuce leaves were wilted. Brown. Ugly. And the carrots were wrinkled, dried up. Pale in color. There was really no describing the tomatoes. They looked. . .repulsive. And the broccoli. . .*was* that broccoli? I couldn't quite tell.

"Good evening, ladies." Janetta ushered us a bit closer. "I hope you're hungry tonight. I've worked all afternoon to fix something special. Take a look inside this salad bowl."

As the others gazed inside the bowl, several of the women muttered, "Hope they don't expect us to eat that," and other such things, but Janetta just continued to smile.

"I know that Diedre talked to you about how to keep the plants in our garden strong and healthy. Water, fertilizer, sunlight—all of these things are needed to keep our flowers in tip-top shape. As you can see. . ." —she gestured to the bowl filled with dilapidated lettuce—"I have here, for your viewing pleasure, a bowl filled with wilted veggies. Not very appealing, is it?"

Sheila gave a one word response. "Ugh."

Evelyn stepped in and took over for Janetta. "Now we want to show you a healthy salad, one you're sure to love."

Janetta trotted off to the kitchen and returned carrying a large salad bowl filled with crispy romaine lettuce, bright orange carrots, red and green peppers, fresh cucumber slices, chopped white cauliflower, deep green chunks of broccoli, and ripe, red tomatoes.

"Now that's more like it," Sheila whispered in my ear.

"I'm sure you've already figured out that we're trying to prove a point," Evelyn said. "Everything that comes out of a garden should be healthy. Hearty. The same is true of our spiritual walk. We don't want to end up looking like that bowl of wilted vegetables. The Lord wants us to be strong. Filled with life and energy. Ready to face the world. We'll talk more about that after we've finished eating, and then you'll have a clearer understanding of this little demonstration."

She prayed over the food, and we dove in. I'd never seen—or tasted—a better salad. After we ate, it was time to get down to business. Evelyn had a teaching, one she assured us would cause us all to blossom and grow.

"I heard a great quote once by an artist named Lou Erickson. He said that gardening requires lots of water—most of it in the form of perspiration. I have to agree. We've put a lot of sweat equity into this garden already. But the work we've done would all be in vain if we finished up the garden and then left it alone, untended.

"Likewise, I'd like to talk to you about God, the Master Gardener. Some people have said that the Lord created the world and everything in it—including man—then left it all to its own devices. That He's not a God who's involved in the cares and concerns of His people. Nothing could be further from the truth. If you think of the Lord as a gardener, you'll have a clearer picture of how He works in our lives. He stirs our hearts, plants seeds—the fruit of the spirit, for example—then encourages us to water those seeds so they'll grow. He prunes us. . ."

Sheila groaned and whispered, "Don't I know it."

"God wants us to blossom. To reach our fullest potential. In order to do that, we've got to be fed and watered and receive plenty of sunlight. Our roots have got to go down really deep—and that takes time. Growth doesn't happen overnight. We've got to read the Bible and spend intimate time with God. Bask in His presence. When we gather together to worship, we're doing just that. A well-tended garden is a healthy garden.

"There's a story in the thirteenth chapter of Matthew. We call it the parable of the sower. In this story we read about seeds falling on all sorts of ground. Some fell on rocky soil, and the roots didn't go deep enough. Some fell among thorns and were unfruitful because they were choked off. But here's what the Bible says about the seeds that fell on good soil: " 'The one who received the seed that fell on good soil is the man who hears the word and understands it. He produces a crop, yielding a hundred, sixty or thirty times what was sown.' "

I listened intently to her words, wondering how she might tie this back to our gardening adventure.

"Now, I don't know about you," Evelyn said, "but I want to be a fruit-bearer. I want a good return on my crop. And that means I'm going to have to stay in the Word, reading every day. And my prayer time has to be consistent. Otherwise, I'll begin to wither up. Before long, I'll be as wilted as that lettuce we saw, or as dried up as those stale carrots."

Ouch. I paused to reflect on her words. I'd been so busy these past few weeks that my quiet time had suffered. But I wanted a good return on my crop, too. So I figured I'd better get busy with all of that watering and fertilizing.

"Think of yourself as a little sprout." Diedre smiled. "When you're a baby Christian, you're just a little shoot popping out of the ground. Then as you grow, you're getting sturdier. Stronger. Your roots are going down deeper. You can withstand more. But you won't withstand the elements unless you're fed and watered." She paused and turned the pages in her Bible.

Evelyn took over, sharing her heart. "If you've been feeling dry lately. . .if you're reaching the point where the sun is burning down hot on your shoulders and you're not feeling the cool shade of His presence, then it's time to do something about it. God wants His girls to be healthy. I'm convinced that the Proverbs 31 woman had a good handle on this. Otherwise how could she have accomplished all that she did?"

Evelyn wrapped up the teaching with a lengthy prayer—lengthy in a good way—then instructed us to divide into small groups once more, where we could share our thoughts about today's lesson. I ended up in a group with Diedre, which was another good thing.

We had a great conversation about our spiritual health then prayed for one another.

I left the Bible study that night thinking about everything Diedre had said. My mind reeled as I took it all in. In so many ways, my investigation was like planting a garden. The suspects had planted plenty of clues. Some had even watered them. And tiny shoots had sprung up. Take Roger Kratz. He liked to bake. Had he, perhaps, whipped up a batch of poisoned brownies?

Seeds of suspicion regarding Louise McGillicuddy had certainly blossomed, too, hadn't they? Especially during the past few days. My heart quickened as I thought about the many possibilities.

Instead of fretting, I opted to take these concerns to the Lord—to rest in His shade, as it were. He had the answers to all my questions.

Now if I could only keep those weeds from growing up. . .maybe I could get to the bottom of this.

18

EVERYTHING'S COMING UP ROSES

My cell phone rang early Friday morning. I smiled as I discovered Sheila's number on the caller ID. I answered with a cheerful "You're up early."

"Well, hello and good morning to you, too." She laughed. "I am up early. Had the funniest call from Diedre a few minutes ago. I thought you'd get a kick out of the news."

"News?" I sat straight up in bed, anxiety kicking in. Had there been a break in the investigation? Had O'Henry contacted the family with information? If so, why was I the last to know?

"Calm down, Agatha Annie. This isn't the kind of news you're thinking. But it's news all the same." Sheila paused for a moment. "Thanks to you, Sean has been working with Maggie at the flower shop for the past couple of weeks."

I felt the breath go out of me at her words. So this really had nothing to do with the investigation.

"Yes, I saw his car out front the other day. How's that going?"

Sheila giggled. "Well, let's just say that the Lord knew what He was doing, that's all. Sean has had his eye on Maggie for some time now, according to Diedre."

"No way."

"Way."

"You're saying he's interested in her. . .in a romantic way?"

"Has been for the past couple of years," Sheila explained. "But he wasn't prepared to date her because he was so busy with his schooling. He's one of those perpetual students." She went off on a tangent about his various degrees, and I listened closely, though I wished she'd move on to the good stuff. "Diedre also said he waited because he wasn't sure where Maggie stood with the Lord," Sheila added. "But apparently there's been some progress in that area, too."

"You're kidding."

"Nope. Diedre's been praying and has asked us to do the same. She's wanted Maggie as a daughter-in-law for some time now. And I think it would be fabulous if Diedre got to pick up where Fiona left off. Mothering Maggie, I mean."

"Maggie does seem like a bit of a lost soul," I added. Indeed, whenever I was around her, I sensed she was holding me at arm's length. But why?

"Just think. . ." Sheila giggled. "If Sean and Maggie fall in love and get married, then Maggie will be Candy's sister-in-law."

"Oh, my goodness." I almost dropped the phone at that one. "I hadn't thought of that."

"One more flower in the garden, eh?" Sheila laughed.

She went on to talk about Diedre's hopes for Sean and Maggie, but my thoughts drifted. I still hadn't ruled out Maggie as a suspect, after all. Her behavior over the past few weeks had boggled me. Why had Maggie left town on the very day of Fiona's death?

What was she hiding?

Only one way to know for sure. I had to see her—right away.

After ending the call with Sheila, I decided to pay Maggie an impromptu visit. I pulled up to the front of the flower shop minutes later and put the car in park. Staring at the FLOWERS BY FIONA sign, I sighed. What would Fiona have thought about the goings-on inside? If she knew that the son of her second cousin twice removed was now dating the young woman she'd mentored, would she approve? I would never know. But I did know that the feeling of uneasiness I had around Maggie needed to be dealt with.

I entered the shop, perplexed to find Maggie missing from the front of the store. Again. Instead, I found Sean managing the counter.

"Good morning to you, too, Mrs. P." He greeted me with a smile. "Has there been a change in plans for the wedding?"

"Well, I did need to let Maggie know about something, actually," I responded. "We've lost a groomsman, so that's one less boutonniere to make. And I plan to do more work on the centerpieces than I'd originally thought, so she needs to know that. Now that we're getting down to the wire, I just want to run over our plan of action with her one final time."

"I'll let Maggie know. I'm sure she'll be happy to talk to you when she gets here. She's been in Philly most of the day. I expect her back anytime now."

"Expect *who* back?" A singsong voice rang out from the back room, and Maggie entered with a smile on her face. "I'm here."

Sean's face paled. "It startles me every time she comes in the back way." He looked at her with—what was that, affection?—in his eyes.

Maggie came from around the counter and took me by the hand. "Annie, I hope you have a few minutes to visit. I have something to tell you."

"O—okay."

She led me into the back room, where I found a host of floral-arranging supplies.

"Wow. I've never been back here before. This place is. . ."

"Messy?"

"Well, maybe a little, but I was going to say *crowded*. You guys need more room."

Sean poked his head inside just long enough to say, "I'm working on that," and then disappeared into the front of the shop once more.

I wondered at the joy that filled Maggie's eyes as she looked at Sean. It appeared that something truly had blossomed between the two of them. Love, perhaps? Had Diedre's prayers been answered?

Maggie ushered me to a chair at the back of the room. I sat at her command. She paced the area in front of me, and my heartbeat quickened.

"Can you just tell me?" I asked. "Whatever it is, I can take it." *I hope.*

"Okay." Tears sprang to her eyes. "Oh, Annie, I feel like I've been given a new lease on life. A second chance."

"Y—you have?"

"Yes. I know you've been curious about my trips back and forth to Philly over the past four weeks, and I don't blame you. But here's the deal. . . ." She knelt in front of me and grabbed my hand. "A couple of months ago, I got a bad report from the doctor."

"A bad report?" At once my hands began to shake. Maggie was too young for a bad report. . .wasn't she?

"During a routine examination, my OB/GYN found a lump in my right breast."

"Oh, Maggie, I'm so sorry."

"I was scared," Maggie confessed, "in part because I saw the concern in my doctor's eyes. I'm thirty-eight. Should've already had my first mammogram at thirty-five, but I put it off. So she sent me for one."

"In Philly."

"Yes." Maggie nodded. "And they found the spot, all right. So from there, they scheduled an ultrasound. Also in Philly."

It was starting to make perfect sense to me now— why Fiona had made the run to Moyer's that fateful day. Why I'd seen the CLOSED sign on the door of the flower shop so often these past few weeks.

"After the ultrasound, the doctors were suspicious enough that they felt I needed a biopsy, which I had last week," she explained.

I reached to give her hand a squeeze. "I wish I had known. I would've gone with you."

Tears rose to cover her lashes. "This is when I miss Fiona the most," she admitted. "She would've been right here beside me all the way. I've missed having that person in my life."

I made up my mind in that instant to be that person in her life. I'd planted seeds of friendship, and now I'd water them and watch them grow. I'd stick with her no matter what. Whether she married into the Caine family or not.

"I've been waiting to hear the results of the biopsy," she said. "And trust me, it was a tough wait. But. . ." Her face lit into a smile. "I just got the news. It's not cancer. The doctor said I have fibrocystic breasts. Not great news but certainly better than the alternative. I'll have to go in for mammograms routinely, but. . ." Her eyes filled with tears again. "I've been given a reprieve."

Wrapping her in my arms came naturally. I felt like shouting, like calling the governor and thanking him for the eleventh-hour stay. Instead, I did what came naturally. I began to pray. I wasn't sure how Maggie would take to my outburst but didn't pause to think much about it. Instead, I let the words flow. I thanked God for His grace and mercy, thanked Him for this excellent news, and thanked Him for my new friend.

When I reached the end of my prayer, I heard a masculine "Amen" join in with mine and looked up to see Sean's smiling face.

"Hope you don't mind that I barged in." He reached for Maggie's hand. "But I have a vested interest in Maggie's health." He reached over to give her a warm hug. A long hug. A hug that involved a few tears and soft whispers in her ear.

"Wow." So Sheila had it right. These two were actually in love. I looked back and forth between them, marveling at how the Lord had worked out all the details. And in such short order. I'd been so wrong about Maggie.

I let that realization sink in. I'd been wrong about her and could have missed an opportunity to be her friend. I needed to remedy that right away.

I exhaled and then spurted out my thoughts. "Maggie, I can't leave here without saying one more thing."

"What's that?"

"I don't ever want to see you go through anything by yourself again. That's why the church is here, to walk through the valleys with you and to celebrate your victories alongside you. I want you to promise me"—tears filled my eyes as I spoke—"that you will come back to church. Let us be there for you."

Maggie laughed. "Trust me, I'm coming. Sean's got me convinced that I should." She sighed. "I don't know what took me so long, to be honest. Just so much healing that needed to be done in my life."

Tilling.

"I've had a lot of hurts from the past," she explained. "And I can't begin to tell you about the guilt I've felt."

"Guilt?"

"Yes." Her chin began to quiver as she explained. "If I hadn't been at the doctor's office that day, Fiona never would have gone to Moyer's. I would have gone." She sighed. "And I can absolutely assure you I wouldn't have touched any brownies. I'm on a diet. So everything would have been fine. Absolutely everything." A lone tear dribbled down her cheek, and she brushed it away.

"Maggie." I took her by the hand. "Only God knows the number of our days. We can't question why Fiona's not with us anymore. All we can do is thank Him for the time we have left. We don't look back. We only look forward."

"That's right." Sean pulled her into his arms and planted kisses in her hair. "The sadness is behind you now. From now on. . ." He paused and seemed to be pondering his next words.

"Everything's coming up roses?" I offered.

Maggie laughed. "That's perfect, Annie. Yes, everything's coming up roses. I'm sure there will be a few weeds, too, but we can deal with them. . ." She gazed into Sean's eyes. "Together."

19

FORGET-ME-NOT

O n Saturday morning, just one week before the big day, Sheila and I agreed to meet at The Liberty Belle so that she could have her roots done and I could get a brand-new 'do'. Though I would never admit it to a living soul, I had some reservations about Candy working on my hair. I'd been in that position once or twice before with a newbie clipping away. . .slowly, slowly, slowly. The results had been frightening, to say the least. But Candy insisted. She wanted to make me over for her wedding, and who was I to stop the bride-to-be?

I pulled into the parking lot at 9:15 and took note of the fact that Sheila had not yet arrived. I decided to go on inside and get this ball rolling. As I entered the salon, the pungent odor of perm solution sent my nose hairs into a tailspin. I noticed Evelyn in the chair closest to the window, gabbing with her stylist as her hair was wrapped in foils. I paused to say hello as I passed by then noticed the sign at the stylist's station: LET ME GIVE YOU A HAIRDO TO *DYE* FOR. *Cute.*

At the next booth a woman with a towel wrapped around her hair was just taking her seat. The distinct smell of perm solution radiated from her head. She leaned her face forward to pull off the towel, and I prepared myself for the full brunt of the odor. The stylist, an older woman named Bonnie I'd known for years, turned to offer a smile, but I found myself distracted by the sign in front of her chair that read, SUCH A TEASE!

I started to say something funny in response but found my tongue stuck to the roof of my mouth as the woman in the chair lifted her head. The reflection in the mirror did not lie. Gloria Moyer. Eddie's wife. What in the world was she doing here, at The Liberty Belle, getting a perm? Washing that man right out of her hair, perhaps? Why? How? With Eddie missing, she should be out combing the fields—pun intended—not having a cut and curl.

I did my best not to draw attention to myself as I slipped off to Candy's seat near the back of the salon.

"Hey, Mom!" She greeted me with a hug then gestured for me to sit, which I did.

"Hi, baby." I grabbed a magazine and hid behind it.

"What do you think of my sign?" She pointed to a framed piece of paper that read, I'M A BEAUTICIAN, NOT A MAGICIAN.

I couldn't help but laugh. "I hope you're not saying I *need* a magician."

"No, Mom." She ran her fingers through my hair. "You don't need a magician, but you are long overdue for a change."

"I am?"

"Mm-hmm."

"W–what kind of change?" After all, I'd worn my hair pretty much the same way for years. Noticing the magazine slipping, I lifted it back up again, hoping Gloria couldn't see me.

"Oh, I just thought we might. . ." Candy's voice

trailed off, and she gave me a curious look. "Mom, what are you doing?"

"Nothing. Just give me a minute."

I started to give her a heads-up when I heard a voice ring out across the salon. "Yoo-hoo! Anybody home?"

Sheila. Great.

As always, she came in with a bang. I peeked above the top of my magazine to let her know where to find me then waved my hand in the air, hoping she'd take the hint. No such luck.

"Who ya hidin' from, Annie Peterson?" she called out. A resounding laugh followed, and I slapped her with my magazine when she got close enough to do so.

At this point, Gloria turned to me with a stunned expression. Her cheeks flamed pink as she stammered, "Well, hello, Mrs. Peterson, I. . ."

"Oh, is this a friend I haven't met?" Sheila, always ready to make a new friend, turned toward the flustered Mrs. Moyer with great zeal.

"She's. . ." I stumbled over the word, realizing for the first time that Sheila had never actually laid eyes on Gloria. Heard about her, sure. Seen her, no. Boy, would I have a hard time explaining this later.

Sheila sashayed across the room and stuck out her hand. "I'm Sheila, Annie's best friend."

"G–Gloria Moyer."

Now, I have to admit, I was watching all this from behind the magazine, which I'd picked up once again. Even with my best peeking skills, I couldn't make out Sheila's face. But her body position changed the minute Gloria's name was spoken. She withdrew her hand and grew eerily silent—something that rarely happened.

I turned back to face Candy, the magazine now trembling in my hand.

"Mom, what's going on?" she whispered. "Who is that woman?"

"Shh." A firm shake of my head let her know I'd rather not discuss it right now, thank you very much, but she refused to let it go.

"Is she a suspect?"

I released a groan. How could a respectable super-sleuth possibly solve a crime with friends and family members getting in the way?

"Yes," I whispered. "Let's talk about it later."

I looked over the top of my magazine again and noticed that Sheila had returned. "You should've told me," she said in a hoarse whisper.

I hadn't spent much time thinking of Gloria as a suspect, but perhaps I should have. Eddie was missing, after all. And what sort of wife went to the hair salon with her husband's whereabouts unknown? Likely she'd driven over from Wallop, hoping no one would figure out what she was up to.

Looked like Sheila was determined to find out. My never-knew-a-stranger best friend moseyed over to Gloria once more, settling into the empty seat beside her. Striking up a conversation just came naturally to Sheila. She could talk a blue streak. Gloria appeared to be flustered as Sheila peppered her with questions: "How long have you lived in the area?" "What do you do for a living?" "Where did you get that lovely blouse?" and so forth. I knew she was buttering her up. Trying to get her to talk.

I lifted the magazine once again and whispered, "What *is* she doing?"

"If you mean Sheila, she's running interference," Candy whispered in response. "If you mean the lady with the red hair, it looks like she's getting a perm. But I think she'd look better with straight hair, to be honest."

Thankfully Candy decided the time had come to whisk me off to the back room to shampoo my hair. Once there, we were finally free to talk. I made her promise she wouldn't share this information with anyone else. Except Garrett, of course. And I also made her promise that she wouldn't worry about me. I felt compelled to add this last part when I saw the wrinkles on her forehead.

Giving her my most convincing look, I took a vow. "I promise I will not let this come before your wedding. This is your week, and I plan to spend it pouring myself out. . .for you."

"Mom." She crossed her arms at her chest and glared at me. "You've spent your entire life pouring yourself out for me. And don't forget, I loved Fiona, too. I'm marrying into her family. No, I don't want to lose you to this investigation the week of my wedding, but if any clues arise, I expect you to go after them. The wedding is going to happen one way or the other. And besides, most of the hard work is done."

Oh, if only you knew, honey. The hard part is watching your daughter walk up the aisle and take the hand—and name—of the man she loves. There's nothing easy about that. Satisfying, yes. Spiritually fulfilling, of course. But easy? Never.

Not that we were exactly ready for the wedding.

There was still work to be done in the courtyard—tables to be set up, centerpieces to make, and so on. And I still had to figure out if I could fit into my mother-of-the-bride dress. The previous weeks had not been good to me. Or, rather, I hadn't been good to them. Regardless, I needed to keep my eye on the goal. Steer away from the investigation for a few days. . .and toward my daughter. Oh, if only Gloria hadn't stumbled into the shop today of all days!

"I want to be fully devoted to you this week," I explained. "To make it the most special time of your life."

"I love you, Mom."

"You, too," I managed past the lump in my throat.

As she led me back into the front room of the salon, I gave her specific instructions to go easy on my hair. "Just a few highlights," I admonished her, "and don't cut too much off the length. I don't want to look like a boy."

"Mom, I'm not going to do anything crazy."

She started by putting the color in my hair, adding the foil wraps. When she finished up with that process, which involved rinsing out any traces of odor and commenting on her great color choice, she reached for the scissors. My stomach flip-flopped. In part because I wondered what she might do to me and in part because Sheila seemed to have taken a liking to Gloria Moyer. If I didn't watch out, my best friend might very well end up with divided loyalties. I gave her a "Watch what you're doing" look, but I don't think she noticed. Instead, she and the very somber Mrs. Moyer leaned in toward each other in quiet conversation. Quite suspicious.

Several minutes later, just as Candy took the last snip with the scissors, Gloria rose from her chair, hair-do complete. I had to admit, she looked great, in spite of Candy's earlier speculations. For the first time, I noticed her red-rimmed eyes. Saw the dark circles underneath. I noticed the trembling in her hands and the quiver in her voice as she said good-bye.

After she left, Sheila headed back my way, shaking her head. "I'll tell you what," she said. "I feel so sorry for that woman. She's going through so much right now."

"Mm-hmm."

"What?"

"Nothing. Just be careful. She could be pulling the wool over your eyes."

Candy turned on the blow-dryer and went to work on my hair. Sheila's voice raised loud enough for everyone within a mile or two to hear her.

"Annie, she had a perfectly reasonable excuse for coming to Clarksborough. Her mother lives in the new retirement community at the end of Main, and she comes here every morning to see her. Besides that, she said her hairdresser over in Wallop is out of town. Someone local recommended The Liberty Belle."

"Ah." I'd have to check into all that.

"I know what you're thinking."

"What?" I raised the level of my voice to match Sheila's.

"You think maybe she baked those brownies."

"Maybe." I shrugged. "She certainly knew enough about Louise's habits to know just what to bake and where to put them."

"You think maybe she's the reason her husband is

missing now, too. Maybe she's done something to him. Wants his life insurance or something like that."

"Maybe."

"And you think she's not acting much like a grieving wife."

"Bingo." I ignored the stares of the others in the room and focused on Sheila. "Anything else?"

"Just a gut feeling." She dropped into the chair next to me. "Whenever I look at her, I think about those flowers we planted."

"You do?"

"Yeah. She's pretty fragile right now. Needs some TLC. But with a little bit of water and sunshine, she might just blossom into someone we could love."

"Humph. She's just too. . .too. . ."

"Perfect?"

"Yes." That was it, exactly. She lived the ideal life. Great looks. Rich husband. Expensive farmhouse in Wallop. The picture-perfect existence.

Hmm. Was I jealous of Gloria, perchance? Had I grown to suspect her because I felt, in some way, that she didn't deserve such an easy, perfect life?

"What are you going to do if she turns out to be completely innocent?" Sheila jabbed.

"I don't know, Sheila." I really didn't want to think about that right now. I needed to work this through in my head. Maybe Gloria wasn't guilty of anything, but I wouldn't know unless I spent a little time investigating and a lot of time praying.

Candy, who'd been quietly styling my hair, shut off the blow-dryer and turned to me with a smile. "What do you think, Mom?"

In all the chaos, I'd forgotten about my hair. I stared in the mirror at my stylish new hairdo, completely won over by my daughter's handiwork. Running my fingers through the choppy blond over brown strands, I had to admit, it looked pretty good. No, not *pretty* good. *Really* good.

"Honey, it's perfect!"

I stared at my reflection for another moment, noticing the wrinkles around my eyes and the ever-present double chin. Even the new hairstyle couldn't wipe those things away. No, I couldn't turn back the hands of time. And no, I would never look like Evelyn. Or Diedre. Or Gloria, for that matter. I wouldn't have perfect hair, glistening teeth, and flawless skin. But as I contemplated the image in the mirror—the unique flower God had created—I suddenly realized that I was exactly who He had made me to be.

Looking into Sheila's face, as I remembered what she had to say about Gloria, the thought occurred to me. . .maybe she was just a grieving wife who'd come to Clarksborough to visit her elderly mother. Maybe the loss of her first husband had caused more pain than I knew. And maybe she was missing Eddie like crazy.

If only I didn't have so much to do this week, I'd get busy trying to figure it all out. But looking at my daughter's beaming face, pondering our conversation about her big day, I realized I'd better stay focused on the task at hand. After all, investigations would come and go. My daughter would only get married once. And that once-in-a-lifetime wedding. . .was only seven days away.

20

Picking Wildflowers

I spent Monday and Tuesday in overdrive working on wedding stuff. On Wednesday morning, when things slowed down a bit, I decided to call O'Henry. I wanted to tell him about my run-in with Gloria Moyer and ask a few questions. Had he been tailing her? Did he already know she'd ventured to Clarksborough?

Perhaps the biggest question of all, however, was, Would O'Henry even talk to me? As he'd already mentioned, I wasn't on the Clark County payroll. I really had no vested interest here, save my friendship with Fiona. And I knew him to be pretty tight-lipped about unsolved cases. What could I do to entice the good sergeant to open up?

Ah yes. Perhaps a good hot meal was in order. The diner on Main featured Philly cheesesteak on Wednesday. I had it on good authority that O'Henry loved a good Philly cheesesteak, so I telephoned him at once and asked if he'd like to meet me there during his lunch break.

He arrived in uniform, informing me that he only had forty-five minutes to eat, chat, and get back to work. I didn't mind. Ten minutes would've been enough. I just needed to get to the bottom of a few things. Our waitress appeared, taking our drink orders and returning shortly with them in hand. After that, we both instructed her to return forthwith with our

Philly cheesesteak sandwiches. She flashed a smile and promised to do just that.

O'Henry doctored his coffee and took a tentative sip. "So, let's cut to the chase, Annie," he said. "I can't imagine that this invitation to lunch isn't without some strings attached."

I shrugged. "You know me pretty well."

"Don't you have a wedding coming up this week? Shouldn't you be hemming bridesmaids' dresses or baking a wedding cake or something?" He dumped another packet of sugar into the coffee then gave it a stir with his spoon.

"I did promise Candy I'd try not to let anything interfere with her big day. That's why I wanted to talk to you, actually. Just to put my mind at ease so I can let this thing go. I just have a couple of questions and then I'm done with this thing. Kaput. Over. Finished." As if to prove the point, I lifted my glass of diet soda in a celebratory manner then took a swig.

O'Henry appeared to relax. "Well then, ask away."

"Have you been keeping tabs on Gloria Moyer?"

"Like, do I know she comes to Clarksborough several days a week to see her mom at the retirement home?" he asked. "And that she ran into you at The Liberty Belle on Saturday morning?" He gave me a scrutinizing glance. "Nice hairdo, by the way. Forgot to mention it earlier."

"Thanks. So, you don't find Gloria's actions suspect? I mean, what if she married Moyer. . ."

"For his money?"

"Yes."

"Nope. She came into the marriage with plenty of money from her first marriage. And they signed a prenup. She showed it to me herself."

"Wow." I took another swallow of my diet soda then leaned back against the booth. "Do you have any idea how her first husband died?"

"We *all* know how he died, Annie. It was in the papers for days. Quite a big deal. He was the owner of the *Clark County Gazette*, you know. And the *Wallop Examiner*."

"Jeffrey Harkins?"

"Yes, she was Mrs. Jeffrey Harkins until he passed away less than a year ago. Aortic dissection. He collapsed in his office and died before he even reached the hospital. The autopsy results were indisputable."

"Are you sure? Because Fiona died very quickly, too, so. . ."

"Annie, listen." O'Henry reached over and patted my hand. "I know you want to figure this out. We all do. But you've got to leave this to the pros. We're on the job. Gloria has been ruled out as a suspect. She's just a woman with a lot of money who married a second husband who also happened to have a lot of money. Maybe she remarried him a little sooner than she should have. Maybe people are speculating. She was a lonely female who didn't know how to function alone. I see that a lot."

"But Eddie has disappeared," I reminded him. "And he just happened to have a plate of poisonous brownies on his desk. You're telling me you don't even suspect that she could have been the one behind it all?"

"From what I hear, Gloria wouldn't know how to

bake a batch of brownies if her life depended on it. She's always had people to do that sort of thing for her. And I can assure you she's been closely tailed since Eddie's disappearance. She's not the one we're looking for. And whether you choose to believe it or not, she's more worked up about his disappearance than all the rest of us put together."

"So worked up that she drove to Clarksborough to get her hair done?"

"I told her to get back to her normal life." O'Henry took a swig of his coffee. "Told her that staying cooped up in her house wasn't going to bring him back any quicker. I even suggested The Liberty Belle when I heard she was coming to town to see her mom."

Ah. Well, I guess that made sense. "Let's shift gears," I suggested. "What about Roger Kratz?"

O'Henry started to respond, but the waitress showed up at our table, sandwiches in hand.

After she left, he said, "I'll admit, Kratz looked like a viable suspect from the start. He had motive. He was mad at Moyer for overcharging him and even madder that his wife's jewels were pawned."

"So?"

"So, we checked out his whereabouts on the week of Fiona's death. He was in Ohio at his daughter's house."

"But he called Moyer's the day after Fiona's death. I know because I was there."

"I know it, too." O'Henry looked exasperated. "Louise called me that same evening. Told me all about it. She's been suspicious of him from the get-go. But that call was made from a 513 area code. Ohio, Annie.

He's been ruled out as a suspect."

"Well, let's talk about Eddie, then. Do you think he pawned Kratz's wife's jewels?"

"I haven't gotten to the bottom of that, to be perfectly honest. And even if I had, I wouldn't share that information with you. It's one thing to talk about a suspect who's been absolved; it's another to leak information on someone still under investigation."

"So Moyer's still under investigation then. You think maybe he disappeared because he has something to hide."

"Annie. Let's not do this."

I gave him an imploring look. "C'mon, Michael. I was your Sunday school teacher, for pete's sake. Watched you pull pranks on Pastor Miller during his sermons. And you're telling me you can't even—"

"Nope. I can't." O'Henry reached for his Philly cheesesteak sandwich and pressed it into his mouth. After a few bites, he turned the questions around on me. "So how are the wedding plans coming?"

"Fine."

"And your parents? They're coming from Mississippi?"

"Of course. They'll arrive on Friday afternoon." I'd been looking forward to it for weeks, in fact. My Southern belle mama would be a fine asset on the wedding day.

Somehow the sergeant, brilliant strategist that he was, ate up the rest of our time, both literally and figuratively. He got me distracted, talking about the garden at church. By the time the check arrived, he knew far more about me and my daughter's wedding than I knew about the case. *I don't know how you do it,*

Sarge, but you've got a gift.

As I made the drive back to the house, I thought through the case one last time, determined to release it as soon as a few lingering questions were answered. If O'Henry had ruled out both Gloria and Roger, then we were really down to three suspects: Louise McGillicuddy, Jim Roever, and Eddie Moyer. Any one of them could have done the deed. But since I'd promised my daughter not to let anything interfere with her wedding, I needed to let sleeping dogs lie. Maybe next week after I'd rested I could dive back in. For now, I just needed to keep my eye on the goal: my daughter's wedding.

I managed to spend a quiet afternoon at home, focused on the things I should be focused on. I put together several centerpieces for the reception. Afterward, I wrapped plastic silverware in colorful napkins and tied them off with ribbons and silk daisies. At 4:40 I looked up at the clock, stunned to see how quickly the afternoon had passed. I needed to get to the church in a hurry. I couldn't bear to miss this last Bible study in the garden.

I arrived at the church at five o'clock, anxious to get started. Knowing this was the last time we'd all work together on this project made it bittersweet.

Within minutes the other women arrived. Sheila arrived on her own, with no chauffeur this time around. She'd pulled her hair up in her DIGGER cap, and her T-shirt was so covered in dirt smudges that I could hardly make out the words underneath.

I found something else funny, too. In all the years I'd known Sheila, I couldn't recall ever seeing her without makeup, but today. . .I stared at her face in disbelief. Except for a bit of smudged mascara, which looked like it had been applied yesterday, she didn't have a bit of color on her face. Except that which God had given her, of course.

"How's the garden coming?" I asked.

Her face lit in a glorious smile, and suddenly the color she'd been lacking from blusher and lipstick appeared quite naturally. "Oh, Annie! Orin and I are having the time of our lives. We're going to Philly next week to the arboretum. You and Warren should really come with us." Her blue eyes sparkled, and I realized she didn't even need the eyeliner.

We talked at length about her gardening project; then Diedre clapped her hands to get our attention. We gathered around and I noticed she held a large bottle in her hand with the word PESTO-MATIC emblazoned on the side.

"Today we're talking about bugs and pests," Diedre started.

I half expected to hear Sheila whine about the topic, but instead she leaned over and surprised me by whispering, "I spent three hours on the Internet this week researching this very thing."

Wow.

"Imagine you've planted a beautiful garden." Diedre gestured to the courtyard area. "You water those little babies, tend to them carefully, weed around them, and add fertilizer. Then one day you come out to the garden and discover that the leaves are speckled with brown spots. The problem starts out small, but then it grows. By the next week, the whole garden is infested with pests."

Ah. I had a feeling I knew where she was going with this.

"The Bible says we've got to watch out for little foxes that spoil the vine," she said. "My little foxes might be different from your little foxes, but they're all pests just the same. For some of us, work-related problems can get in the way of our relationship with the Master Gardener. For others, our habits—too much time on the Internet, excessive television watching, overeating—start to take over. Before we know it, our quiet time is zapped away with unnecessary things."

Like a crime I don't really have time to solve.

"Whatever pests you're struggling with today, the Lord wants you to acknowledge them as the distractions they are. He wants you to be wholly surrendered to him. He's not interested in 10 percent of your time. He wants all of you—24/7."

"We're going to talk more about this after dinner," Evelyn interjected. "But in the meantime, we've got some work to do. We want our gardens to be pest-free, so we're going to divide into groups and cover all the areas with pesticide."

I didn't want to think about the investigation, especially after Evelyn's admonition, but somehow the word *pesticide* got me to thinking about Fiona Kelly. Thinking about Fiona got me to thinking about Maggie and Sean. Thinking of Maggie and Sean shifted my thoughts to Diedre. And looking at Diedre—who now stood in front of me holding a bottle of Pesto-Matic in her hand—made me wonder if I was doomed to distraction. Were these little pests that sent my thoughts reeling *ever* going to disappear?

"We're going to start by talking about the daisies. They are affected by a couple of pests in particular—aphids and whiteflies."

"Whiteflies are terrible," Sheila whispered. "I've been reading up on them."

"You have?" Was she joking? Trying to put a bug in my ear? Er, trying to distract me?

"Yes. You can find out if you have a whitefly problem by looking at the back of the leaves. If you find spots, then you need a pesticide."

"Like Pesto-Matic?" I stressed the syllables as if I were advertising the product on a television commercial.

"Yes."

We went to work, ridding our garden of pests—the itsy-bitsy flying kind, anyway—and then, after thoroughly scrubbing our hands, went into the fellowship hall for our last gardening meal together. I could sense a quick sadness over the room as we all realized that our teaching was coming to an end. I thought about that first Wednesday night—was it really four weeks ago?—when Evelyn had given us the news about the gardening project. My enthusiasm level had left something to be desired. But tonight. . . tonight I had to admit, I'd fallen in love with not only the flowers, but the process. And I'd learned a lot, too. What was it Evelyn had said again? Ah yes. I'd learned . . .about life, gardening, and womanhood.

Now if I could just figure out how to pull off my daughter's wedding without letting my investigation get in the way. . .*that* would truly be an accomplishment. Looked like I was going to need several cases of Pesto-Matic!

21

Down the Garden Path

On the Thursday before the wedding, I raced around the house, preparing for my parents' arrival the next day. The sheets on the guest bed needed to be washed, and the bathroom, which they would share with Devin, needed some work.

Around five o'clock the telephone rang. The caller ID showed a number I didn't see very often—Garrett's. I answered with a smile.

"Hey, you. Hope you're not calling to say you've decided not to go through with it."

A laugh followed on his end. "No, I can assure you I'm going through with it. I'm calling for a completely different reason."

"Oh? What's up?" As I took a seat on the sofa, curiosity settled in.

"I just left Wallop," he explained. "I had a service call at the home of a woman whose hard drive had gone out on her computer."

"All the way over in Wallop?" I queried. Usually his calls were closer to home.

"Yes, this was a referral," he explained. "She said she heard about me through Maggie Preston."

"Ah, I see." I leaned back against the cushions, getting comfortable.

"Anyway, the strangest thing. . ." He hesitated for a moment, and I wondered what might come next.

"This woman had a dog that looked a lot like, well, like Sasha."

I sat straight up. "W–what?"

"I can't be sure." His words came a little faster this time. "But the dog had exactly the same coloring and the same tip of brown at the end of her tail. She had on a different collar and was a lot heavier. Really chubby, in fact."

"Ah." So maybe it wasn't my Sasha.

"The woman called her by a different name, but she didn't really respond well to it."

"What name?" I rose from the couch and began to pace the room.

"Hmm. Let me think." After a moment he said, "I think she called her Ruby."

"Ruby?" Hmm. "And you're sure the dog was the same color?"

"Yes, but there was more to it than that," he said. "The dog seemed to know me. Came right up to me. And you know dachshunds. . .they usually hesitate before making friends. She wagged her tail and got all worked up. I didn't know what to think."

"Who was this woman?"

"Interesting last name," he said. "McGillicuddy."

"Louise McGillicuddy?" I could hardly get the words out; my tongue stuck to the roof of my mouth.

"Yes, that's right. You know her?"

"Oh, I know her all right." At that moment, I slipped over into the white zone. My ears started ringing. My vision turned cloudy. I needed to end this call and drive to Wallop—immediately.

Deep breath, Annie. Deep breath.

It took me approximately sixty seconds to copy down Louise's address, grab my keys and purse, punch Warren's number into the cell phone, and make my way out to the car. By the time I started the ignition, I had both my husband's blessing and his promise to pray.

"Call me as soon as you know something," he said.

The usual thirty-minute trip to Wallop took me twenty-six, to be precise. Knowing I was hot on the trail of my canine companion made my foot a little heavy on the accelerator. All the way, I prayed. Asked the Lord for His perfect will. Asked Him to give me peace, whether the dog turned out to be Sasha or not. I added an extra prayer for grace, not for myself, but for Louise. If she had, in fact, turned out to be the one who'd stolen Sasha.

My prayer time helped calm my nerves, but I still had some unanswered questions lingering in the back of my mind. If Louise could take someone else's property, was she capable of more, perhaps? Like kidnapping Eddie Moyer? Holding him hostage? Despite her arguments to the contrary, had the jilted Ms. McGillicuddy baked the poisoned brownies, hoping that Eddie would eat them? Was she really that vindictive?

Several different scenarios played out in my imagination, but I did my best to squelch them. Until I saw her face-to-face. . .until I knew for sure if she'd taken Sasha. . .all of my ponderings were just that. Ponderings.

I arrived at Louise McGillicuddy's home and rapped on the door, guarding my breaths, which seemed to be coming in rapid succession. Perhaps I should've invited O'Henry to join me. After all, once Louise realized I was on her trail, she might turn on me.

From inside, I could hear barking. Familiar barking. Seconds later, the door opened. I stared into the eyes of one Louise McGillicuddy, holding, in her arms, my baby. The startled woman's eyes widened and she paled as she saw me.

"Mrs. Peterson? W–what are you doing here? And how did you get my address?"

Immediately Sasha went absolutely berserk. The cries were almost unbearable, both from me and my beloved baby.

"Sasha!" I ignored Louise's question and reached for the dog, which squirmed in her arms, tail wagging like crazy. Her high-pitched wails nearly broke my heart.

"What do you think you're doing?" Louise stared at me with confusion registering in her eyes. "This is my dog. Ruby."

"No, she's—" Sasha lunged for me, and as she landed in my arms, I took note of a belly as round as a football. "What in the world. . . ?" *Is she. . .pregnant?*

Louise's eyes filled with tears right away and she gestured for me to come inside. I stepped into the foyer of her small home. Sasha licked me all over the face, from one side to the other. I gushed over her, tears now flowing. "I missed you so much, my little baby! I can't believe I've found you. Oh, your daddy's going to be so happy to see you again. And Copper! He's going to flip!"

Louise continued to stare at me as if I'd landed on

her front porch in an alien spaceship. But I didn't care. She had some explaining to do—and quick.

"Before I call the police," I said to her, "I would like to hear how you ended up with my dog and why you didn't respond to the "missing" posters that Jim Roever posted."

"Police? "Missing" posters?" Her brow wrinkled. "There weren't any posters. And why in the world would the police care that I have a dog?"

"Of course there were posters." I stared at her, feeling almost as confused as she looked. "I brought them to Jim Roever at the funeral home weeks ago, the day after Sheila and I met you."

"The same day Jim Roever was fired, you mean?" She shook her head. "Listen, Mrs. Peterson, I found this dog that same day. No collar. She was wandering the cemetery completely lost and frightened. I had no idea who she belonged to, so I put a notice in the local paper."

"Y–you did?" I asked. "The *Clark County Gazette*?"

"No, the *Wallop Examiner*," she explained. "I left my contact information and everything. But no one responded. And after a couple of weeks, I realized that Ruby here was. . .with child." She pointed to Sasha's belly. "And I decided she needed a good home, someone to care for her, and a place for the babies to be born."

I felt the tension in my chest begin to release. Maybe Louise wasn't the criminal I'd made her out to be. Maybe she didn't have Eddie Moyer tied up in a back bedroom. Perhaps she hadn't deliberately taken my lovable pooch. Was she simply a lonely soul who'd taken in my little darling and offered her a place to stay. . .out of genuine kindness?

Now what?

I struggled to know what to say next. Should I offer her some sort of proof that Sasha was indeed mine? She didn't seem convinced, though the pup licked me from ear to ear in a never-ending state of frenzy.

An idea struck. "Louise, my husband and I were offering a five-hundred-dollar reward for Sasha's return." I scrambled to pull my purse from my shoulder, while still holding on to the dog. With one hand around Sasha's round middle and the other digging through the contents of my purse, I came up with the piece of paper I'd folded up. . .one I'd kept with me at all times since Sasha's disappearance. A flyer that read MISSING at the top.

"Look here." I pressed the paper into Louise's hand. "This is a picture of Sasha. It was taken last Christmas. See the dark spot on her tail?" I turned my chubby pooch around so that Louise could see for herself that I had the right dog. "And if you need any other proof, I'm sure the vet would be happy to do blood work. Otherwise, all I have to offer is a few tidbits of information. For example, she doesn't like to go outside when it's raining."

"I learned that the hard way."

"And she insists on sleeping in the bed with us, burrowed under the covers."

"Yep."

"She follows me into the bathroom. I never have a minute to myself."

Louise sighed.

"And she's partial to canned food. Can't stand the dry stuff."

Poor Louise. Her eyes filled with tears. For the first time, I realized I'd be taking Sasha away from someone who genuinely cared for her. This new revelation hit hard. But what could I do about it?

"As I said, we're offering a five-hundred-dollar reward for her return."

Louise shook her head. "No, I couldn't possibly take your money. Keeping her was a privilege." A lone tear slipped down her cheek, and I felt a lump rise in my throat.

"I can't thank you enough." Now I was the one with the misty eyes.

"You might want to know that she had some problems with vomiting a couple of weeks ago," Louise explained. "She'd gotten into my stash of miniature chocolates."

"Been there, done that," I said. "We had to take her to the vet several months ago to have her stomach pumped."

"Well, this wasn't that bad," Louise acknowledged. "She only ate three or four small pieces. I looked it up on the Internet and knew, based on her weight, that the amount she'd eaten hadn't been toxic. But I was concerned enough that I called in sick. Stayed home with her all day. It passed. Literally."

Oh my goodness. Well, that explained why Louise had called in sick, anyway.

She spent a few minutes gathering up some things she'd purchased for the dog. All the while, I tried to work up the courage to ask her one more question before leaving. After all, I'd driven a long way and chances were pretty good we'd never end up in a one-on-one conversation like this again.

"Um, Louise. . . ?"

She lifted a large bag of food and turned my way. "Yes?"

"Can I ask you a question about Eddie Moyer?"

At once her eyes filled with tears.

Yikes. Tender subject.

"He's been gone for quite some time now. How are you guys getting along without him at the funeral home?"

"It's awful," she whispered. "And Gloria is sure I'm to blame. Just the thought that anyone suspects me of such a thing makes me feel sick inside. I could never hurt Eddie. Never." Her tears came in force now.

"So where is he, do you think?" I asked. "Do you think he's missing at all, or is he hiding out?"

Her gaze shifted to the ground.

"I know about the pawned jewels, Louise."

Her face paled, and for a moment I thought she might actually faint. "So. . .it's true?"

"Are you saying you didn't know that Eddie was pawning jewels of the deceased?"

"Well, I knew that Kratz accused him, but there was never any proof. And Kratz was always such a strange bird, anyway. He hated Eddie almost from the beginning. I really think it was the pain of his loss. Made him a little crazy. We see a lot of that in this business."

I reached out to take Louise's hand. I knew she didn't want to think badly of Eddie, but I had to ask another question. "I hate to bring this up," I said. "But do you think it's possible that Jim Roever found out

Eddie was stealing the jewels? Maybe that's why Eddie fired him—because he knew too much?"

"I don't know." Louise's dabbed at her eyes. "I've thought about this from so many angles. I just know that a couple of days after Fiona died, Eddie and Jim had an argument in Eddie's office. It was late in the day, thank goodness, because they got pretty loud."

"Do you know what they were arguing over?" I asked. "Was it about the tree?"

"Tree?" She gave me a curious look. "I don't know anything about a tree. I just know that Eddie was pretty red-faced when he came out of the office. Told Jim he was going to call O'Henry." After a pause, Louise added, "Why Eddie wanted to involve the police, I have no idea."

Hmm. So Eddie had threatened to involve the police. Just a slick move on his part to throw off suspicion? Or was there really some reason to think that Jim Roever might have something to do with this?

My gut told me I needed to make one more trip to the cemetery, that my answer would be found there.

22

I Come to the Garden Alone

There's something about driving with a pregnant dog in your lap that makes steering difficult. Several times in the ten-minute trip from Louise's house to the cemetery, I tried to convince Sasha that she'd be better off sitting in the passenger seat. Several times she declined. I didn't mind holding her, really. I just needed to make sure I actually made it to the cemetery. Alive. In one piece.

As I pulled into the cemetery, I eased the car off the road to call Warren. I could hardly wait to tell him I'd found Sasha. When he heard the news, he hollered an uncharacteristic "Praise the Lord!" Then, to my great delight, he asked to speak to her. I put the phone to my little darling's ear and watched her perk up as he showered her with blessings.

"Where are you now, Annie?" Warren asked when I came back on the line.

"Well, I, um. . ."

"Annie." I recognized the stern sound in his voice. Had heard it many times, in fact.

"At the cemetery. I have this niggling suspicion. . . ." My voice trailed off as I contemplated what to say next. How could I explain what didn't even make sense to me?

"Just be careful, honey."

"Of course."

We ended the call, and I slipped the car back into gear. As I made my way down the narrow lane, a light shower started to fall, covering my windshield in tiny droplets. It was one of those comforting rains, the kind that always made me feel like curling up on the sofa with a good book. I knew it wouldn't last long, but I enjoyed it just the same, because I knew our little daisies needed the nourishment. I could use a little myself.

I turned at the first bend in the road, thinking about the significance of the rain. There was something about the drops of water on the blades of grass that tugged at my heart, putting me in mind of something from my past. What had compelled me to come to this place today? Did the Lord have something to share with me, perhaps?

Right away, the lyrics to a song I'd always loved drifted through my mind: *I come to the garden alone, while the dew is still on the roses. And the voice I hear falling on my ear, the Son of God discloses.*

I'd always loved the melody and the somewhat haunting lyrics, but why had they appeared now? Had the Lord led me here, to this gardenlike place? Would He really speak to me? Show me His take on things? As I pondered these questions, more words came. Indisputable words: *He speaks, and the sound of His voice is so sweet the birds hush their singing. And the melody that He gave to me within my heart is ringing.*

I steered the car around the next bend in the road then slowed nearly to a stop so that I could pray. How many little pests had sent my mind reeling over the past few weeks? Likely I'd already missed out on hearing from God several times over simply because of busyness. But no more. "Lord, I don't want anything to distract me from You. . .from Your voice."

I sat in the car with Sasha on my lap until the drizzling rain halted. Then I eased my way out of the car and placed Sasha on the ground, using the leash Louise had given me. I'd keep a close eye on her today. She wouldn't get away, no matter what.

As the two of us walked through the deserted cemetery, more lyrics poured out. I found myself humming at first and then singing. *And He walks with me, and He talks with me, and He tells me I am His own. And the joy we share as we tarry there, none other has ever known.*

Sasha looked up at me, and I smiled. "It's okay, girl. Just keep on walking."

On and on we journeyed, pausing to look at a few of the headstones. Why the Lord had led me here, to a cemetery, was beyond me. I'd simply responded to the call to come. The rest was up to Him, and apparently He was in no hurry today. Odd, in light of the fact that I'd been moving at such a frantic pace over the past several weeks. A message, perhaps, that I should slow down? Spend more time in quiet reflection with Him?

A gentle breeze stirred the air, and a bundle of silk flowers came loose from one of the gravesites nearby. I watched as the wind picked it up and nudged it along. It came to land several inches away from where it started. This served to excite Sasha, who, with tail wagging a mile a minute, led me straight to them.

I knelt to look at the headstone as I put them back in place.

"Jeffrey Harkins." *Wow. Gloria's husband.* The headstone read, BELOVED HUSBAND.

Something about seeing this for myself made it more real. Gloria had lost the man she loved. Sure, she'd married Eddie Moyer, but she had suffered a devastating loss first. How horrible would it be to lose a spouse? I shivered, thinking about it. "Lord, I'm so sorry." I had no right to judge her for how quickly she'd remarried—or anything else, for that matter.

I rose to my feet and let Sasha lead the way as we continued our journey. I had a feeling we were looking for something specific, though I wasn't quite sure what. We strolled for quite some time. I took in the landscaping through new eyes. Jim Roever had done a fabulous job with the plants. And the trees! Some of them looked as if they'd been here for centuries. I noticed a beautiful weeping willow and several sturdy oaks, their leaves a brilliant green. The flowering pear trees took my breath away.

Closing my eyes, I drew in a deep breath and asked the Lord to share His heart with me. Somehow, just being still and quiet seemed to open my spiritual eyes and ears. I could truly sense His presence. I was reminded of Evelyn's story about Moses standing on holy ground. Was it possible, in the middle of a cemetery, to be standing in a holy place? Sure felt that way.

I realized at once that any place I paused to meet with God was holy. A church pew. A garden filled with daisies. A comfy sofa. A cemetery. What mattered most was my willingness to slow down. To linger in His presence. I didn't do that often enough.

The sun glowed a warm orange, reminding me that afternoon had slipped over into evening. Still, I didn't feel compelled to leave. Not yet. Again, I started to hum the old hymn, and before long, more words had slipped out. *I'd stay in the garden with Him, though the night around me be falling. But He bids me go; through the voice of woe, His voice to me is calling.*

I paused, looking up once again at the trees. A fabulous silver maple took my breath away. To its right, a row of forsythia bushes.

Hmm. . .
Weeping willow
Oak
Silver maple
Flowering pear
Forsythia

My hands began to tremble as the realization set in. Something was missing from the equation. What was it Jim Roever had said to me over the phone? He'd been fired because of a dispute with Eddie Moyer . . .over a tree. But what kind of tree again? A list of possibilities flitted through my mind, but none of them sounded just right.

I snapped my fingers, suddenly remembering. "The eastern hemlock. Our state tree."

At once I began to search the area, hoping to find it. Where was it? I racked my brain. Ah yes. The center of the property. All I had to do now was find it. To put my mind at ease. To still this sudden lurching in my heart. With renewed energy, I picked up my pace. "C'mon, Sasha. We're on a search for a tree."

Over the next several minutes I walked from one

area of the cemetery to another in search of that elusive tree. In the center of the property, I found several lovely shade trees, none of them eastern hemlocks. In the outlying perimeters, same thing. No eastern hemlock.

Calm down, Annie. Calm down.

Maybe I wasn't looking hard enough. Sometimes the very thing you were looking for was right in front of you.

Circling the grounds one final time, I had to conclude the obvious. "There's no eastern hemlock tree on this property."

The revelation was just that—a revelation. Jim Roever had lied about the eastern hemlock tree. A cold chill wiggled its way down my back, and I pushed back the fear.

If Jim Roever had lied to me about the tree. . .

He'd lied to me about everything.

BACK TO THE GARDEN

I tossed and turned all night Thursday night. When Friday morning dawned bright and clear, my thoughts seemed brighter and clearer. I had a pretty good idea what had happened now but needed to get the confirmation in order to move forward.

As Warren left for the bank, I gave him an assignment. A big one.

He looked at me, clearly curious. "And if I get the information you're looking for, then what?"

"Call O'Henry first, and then call me." I didn't want to usurp the good sergeant's authority; I just wanted to get to the bottom of things. And I couldn't stop this nagging feeling that the answer would be found if we would just take action.

Warren promised to "do the deed" as soon as he had a break in his regularly scheduled workday.

I left the house a few minutes later, headed to Philly to pick up my mom and dad at the airport. Meeting them outside the airport was my usual modus operandi, but today I decided to surprise them by going inside. I found them by the baggage carousel. My dad was trying to lift an oversized suitcase, which I recognized as my mother's. As soon as I laid eyes on my sweet mama, my eyes filled with tears. I called out that magic word, "Mom!" and she turned, her face lighting with joy.

"Annie!" She shoved her overnight bag into my

dad's already-too-full arms and sprinted my way with vim and vigor. Not bad for a seventy-two-year-old woman. "I can't believe you came inside to fetch us! Oh, I've missed you! Is everything ready for the wedding? What do you need me to do? I've come prepared to work, so just name it."

I tried to explain that most of the hard work was done, but getting a word in edgewise proved difficult. As my father drew near, he placed the luggage on the ground and wrapped me in his arms. "Good to see you, peanut."

Well, if that didn't make a girl feel young again, nothing would.

We chatted all the way out to the parking garage, and the conversation rolled on as we left the airport, headed back toward Clarksborough. We discussed the wedding plans at length, focusing on tonight's rehearsal and tomorrow's order of events. Then we talked about Devin's high school graduation, which would take place on Sunday afternoon after church.

My cell phone rang, and I almost came out of my skin when I saw Warren's number. I answered with a tentative hello, my hand trembling so hard I almost lost my grip on the phone. "Hey, Annie. Where are you?"

"On the turnpike."

"Okay." He paused. "I did what you asked. Looked up Jim—or James—Roever to see if he had account with one of our bank branches. He does."

"Really?" I almost lost my grip on the phone altogether. "Did you call O'Henry?"

"Yes. Gave him the scoop first, just like you said.

He said he was grateful for the information but didn't seem overly excited."

"Figures. So tell me."

"Roever kept a pretty low, steady balance until a few months ago," Warren explained. "I could see where he'd been depositing his paychecks. Routine stuff. Then, I think it was in the middle of winter, maybe February, the deposits started changing. The usual ones were there, but so were several others, some of them pretty hefty."

"How hefty?"

"Some in the hundreds, some in the thousands. They were pretty random. But it was all adding up. So much so that he opened a savings account, making several online transfers from checking to savings."

"Okay."

"And here's something that might interest you. Several weeks ago he wrote a really large check to an RV dealership in Philly."

"Hmm. Well, he said he wanted to travel. Do you think he's skipped the state?"

"No. He's still in Pennsylvania," Warren explained. "I know because there have been several small purchases made with his debit card over the past week, and they're all local. Well, mostly."

"What do you mean?"

"I see a couple from this week at a gas station out near the lake, in the Groversville area. Just struck me as odd because he'd wandered from Wallop. Seems unusual for someone who's lived such a routine life."

"Not necessarily," I countered. "He's retired now, so he has more free time on his hands. He enjoys fishing, so being that close to the water makes sense."

"Could be. I noticed there were several purchases at fast-food places, also in Groversville near the lake."

"Mm-hmm." *The lake.* Why did that raise red flags? I paused to give it some thought.

Yes!

It hit me at once. Eddie and Gloria Moyer owned a house out on the lake. Maggie had told me as much. But where? Was it possible we would find Roever there? And Moyer, as well?

"Warren, please pray. I'm going to make a couple of calls and get back to you."

"Don't do anything without involving O'Henry, babe."

"I won't."

When I ended the call, my mother looked at me, her eyes widening. "Annie, something's happening?"

"Yes."

"An investigation? Something big?"

"Yes."

I thought for a minute she would go into panic mode, but instead her face lit into a smile. "I *told* your father that coming to Pennsylvania was always an adventure. We're in this with you, honey. Whatever you need us to do, we'll do."

When my dad dittoed her remarks, I added, "Okay. Just remember you said that."

I telephoned Maggie at once, and she gave me Moyer's lake house address. I then gave O'Henry a call. He surprised me with his response.

"I can take it from here, Annie."

"But. . ."

"Just because Jim Roever had some large deposits doesn't mean he killed Fiona."

"But what if he's in Groversville right now with Eddie?"

"Then we'll find him and get to the bottom of this. But you really need to let us—"

"I'd bet my eye teeth he's in Groversville," I interjected, "and I can even give you an address where he's likely staying."

A much humbler O'Henry came back with, "O–oh?"

"Moyer's lake house."

"Annie, we searched the lake house last week. There were no signs of. . ."

"No, not the house itself. The house sits on several acres of land. Prime land. On the lake. What you're looking for is an RV. Find it and you'll find Roever."

I explained my logic, and he agreed to begin the search.

We decided to meet at a gas station in Groversville at two o'clock. I contemplated stopping in Clarksborough to drop off my parents at my house, but from the look in my mom's eyes, she was more than happy to come, too.

As we made our way down one country road and then another, I filled my parents in on everything they'd missed. I could tell from the gleam in my mom's eyes that she didn't mind showing up at a crime scene on her way to the wedding. Didn't bother her at all, she assured me. "In fact," she added, "a Peterson wedding wouldn't be the same without a little adventure first."

I promised her lots of adventure. . .then pointed the car toward Groversville.

24

A FLOWER FELL

We pulled up to the Gas 'n Go in Groversville at two o'clock and found two patrol cars in the parking lot. O'Henry met me at the door of my car. "Keep your cell phone turned on, Annie. I'll call when I'm convinced there'll be no danger. I'll probably need some information from you, anyway. But I can't allow you to come with me just yet."

While O'Henry and the other officers headed off to Moyer's property, I opened the car door and walked inside the store. I couldn't go into a crime-fighting resolution without plenty of artificial sweetener in me. I bought several diet sodas and enough chocolate bars to feed an army of sleuths.

As we waited in the car, my mother grilled me about tonight's rehearsal dinner and tomorrow's garden ceremony. She wanted every detail. I tried to fill the time by consuming massive quantities of chocolate and answering her questions, but my thoughts were elsewhere. When would O'Henry call? What was taking so long?

At ten minutes after three, my cell phone rang. The sarge sounded tense. "C'mon, Annie."

"Are you sure?"

"Yes, and I owe you an apology. But never mind all that right now. Just get over here. Pass the driveway and go another quarter mile then turn in on the dirt road on the left. Take it back about a mile and a half through the trees to the clearing on the edge of the lake. It's pretty rough, so drive carefully."

"Have you called Gloria?"

"I'm doing that right now."

My hands were trembling so hard that I had a difficult time starting the car. Twice I nearly dropped the keys. I finally managed to get the car started, and we hit the road.

I drove past Moyer's house very slowly, looking for the dirt road in question. I let out a whistle as I viewed the beautiful home for the first time. "Wow. Not bad."

Finally locating the narrow road, I turned the car to the left.

"Drive slowly, Annie," my father admonished.

I eased the car down the bumpy makeshift road, dodging trees all the way. After what felt like an eternity, the forest unfolded into an exquisite clearing on our left. In the very center of this breathtaking spot stood the most beautiful eastern hemlock tree I'd ever seen. Just beyond the tree. . .on the edge of the water. . . a midsized RV. With two patrol cars out front.

As we made our way out of the car, I saw one of the officers leading a handcuffed Roever across the clearing toward a patrol car. As Roever and my father passed each other, I once again noticed the similarities. Soft blue eyes. White hair. Wrinkles. Only this time, Roever's eyes held mine in a menacing gaze. Gave me the shivers. Had he really plotted to kill Moyer only to get Fiona instead?

O'Henry stood in the doorway of the RV, talking to another fellow who wore latex gloves and carried a small plastic bottle, which he prepared to place in an evidence bag. Must be the pesticide. I looked a bit closer and saw that it was a white powder. Looked a lot like. . .flour. A chill came over me as I thought about those brownies.

I looked over at O'Henry, who gestured for us to join him in the RV. He ushered me inside, and my parents tagged along behind. Eddie was seated on the sofa dressed in a shabby looking T-shirt and grungy jeans. He had a cell phone in his hand, and even from this distance I could hear the squeals from Gloria on the other end of the line.

My heartbeat skipped to double time. I wanted to give the man a hug, to tell him how sorry I was that I'd ever suspected him of wrongdoing. Instead, I sat on the love seat and waited patiently.

Moyer wrapped up his call in short order then turned to face us. He nodded when he saw me. "Mrs. Peterson, I don't know how I can ever begin to thank you. I didn't think I was ever getting out of this RV alive."

"I'm just glad to see you're okay. You are okay, aren't you?"

"Of course he's not!" My mother shook her head, her eyes filling with tears. "Just look at the poor man. He looks awful."

I nudged her with my elbow, hoping she'd take the hint.

"The timing worked out perfectly," O'Henry explained. "When we arrived, Roever was outside the RV at the water's edge. Fishing. Like he didn't have a care in the world. We swarmed in around him and took him with no trouble."

"And Eddie?"

"There's something about having a loaded gun pressed to your skull that makes a man want to stay indoors," Eddie responded. "Trust me. I wasn't going anywhere. I knew he was armed. I'd tried on more than one occasion to get around him and almost lost my life as a result."

"Thank God you're all right!" My mother fanned herself.

O'Henry pulled out a pen and paper. "Just start at the beginning, Mr. Moyer."

Eddie stood and paced the room, finally pausing to look out the window. "Well, I guess you could say it all started with that tree right there."

My heart lurched as he pointed at the eastern hemlock. So there *was* a tree in the center of this tale, after all. Just not on the cemetery property, as I'd thought. Still, the Lord had used it to lead me here.

"What about the tree?" O'Henry looked confused.

"See, my pop and Jim used to be friends, years ago," Eddie explained. "They'd come out here to our family property—it was just woods back then, no house or anything—and they'd fish. My dad took a liking to Jim and vice versa. I guess they talked about how they were going to spend their retirement years camping out here. . .that sort of thing."

"Okay?" O'Henry continued to scribble in his notepad.

"My dad died a few years back. Fought a long battle with Alzheimer's. Roever swears that my pop promised him this land in his will. Said they'd talked about it dozens of times. But I have a copy of the will, and there's nothing in it about Roever."

"So he felt slighted when your father died?" I offered.

"I guess." Eddie raked his fingers through his messy hair. "Put me in the middle of something mighty uncomfortable, I'll tell you."

"No doubt." O'Henry glanced up at him.

"This property was never used for anything much, so when Gloria and I married a few months ago, we decided to build a lake house here. Thought it would be a great weekend place. But Roever. . ." Eddie released a lingering breath. "He didn't take that news well at all. He changed completely when the house started going up. And that tree. . ." He pointed once again to the eastern hemlock. "I really think it's to blame for most everything. See, I told Roever a couple months back that I wanted to build a boat landing out here by the water. Told him we'd have to do some clearing first. And when I mentioned cutting down the tree, well. . ."

"He flipped out?" I suggested.

"That's putting it mildly. He said that he and my dad had camped under that tree more times than he could count, and I wasn't destroying it. Said it would be over his dead body."

Or Fiona's dead body.

Eddie shook his head. "I thought I got him calmed down. Suggested he search for another patch of land nearby. Something he could build on. Felt sure he'd find some acreage nearly as nice. But nobody was selling."

"Did Jim Roever have the kind of money it would take to buy lakefront property?" I asked.

"Probably not." Eddie shrugged. "But I guess he figured out a way to come up with some."

"Pawning jewels," O'Henry threw in.

"Apparently." Eddie shook his head. "About a month before Fiona died, I got a call from a pawnshop here in Groversville. They were suspicious about a particular piece of jewelry because one of my customers, Roger Kratz, had confronted them. I didn't know anything about any jewels other than what they were telling me," he said, "but I had my suspicions. If anyone at Moyer's had access—besides Louise and me—it'd be Jim. He certainly knows how and when the bodies are transported. And he was plenty mad at me already, as we've already established."

"And had a need for money," I added. "To buy some land."

"Actually"—Moyer released a sigh—"Gloria and I had already planned to loan him the money if he found a piece of property. I guess I should've just told him that. If I had, maybe Fiona would be alive today."

The room grew silent as we all pondered that statement.

"Before long, Kratz was calling the funeral home, confronting me," Eddie continued. "I don't blame him for thinking the worst, but I hadn't done anything. I was suspicious enough to bring Roever into my office and confront him. Didn't come out and accuse him of stealing. Just told him I'd be watching his moves from that point on. He seemed to take it in stride. In fact, his performance that day was so convincing, I thought maybe I'd made a mistake."

"His acting skills are terrific," I concurred.

"He wasn't acting that night two weeks ago when he entered my office with a gun in his hand," Moyer explained. "From the minute he took me hostage till now, I've watched a crazy man at work. He's been absolutely erratic at times. Up one minute, down the next. Fishing one minute, talking about killing me the next. And I knew he had it in him to do it. Fiona had already died, after all, and I knew that poison was meant for me."

"So Roever baked those brownies." I shook my head, trying to absorb all of this news.

"Yep." Eddie said. "And when I think of how close I came to eating one. . ." He shuddered.

Me, too.

Silence permeated the room. I finally broke it with one word. "Ironic."

Everyone looked my way.

"Jim once told me that folks always referred to him as the Grim Reaper."

"Started as a joke," Eddie said, "but it turned out to be. . ."

"Prophetic?" I offered.

At that moment Gloria burst through the front door. She rushed directly into her husband's arms, babbling incoherently. Between the kissing and the shouting, I somehow made out her praises that she'd found him alive. Looked like all of my suspicions about her were unfounded, to say the least. I didn't know when I'd ever seen a woman more relieved or grateful.

Eventually O'Henry was able to get her calmed down, and she took a seat on the sofa next to her husband, exclaiming, "It's a miracle!"

"Yes, Someone must've been looking out for you," I added.

"I have to agree with you there," Moyer said. "I've never been a religious man, but two weeks locked in an RV with an armed crazy man will drive you to your knees. I remember an old expression my daddy used to use. . .something about how there are no atheists in foxholes. I can attest to that."

"Well, amen," I whispered.

I released a sigh of relief. My investigative work was done. Just as quickly, reality hit. I had a wedding rehearsal to attend!

I glanced down at my watch and gasped. 4:45? By the time we made it back to Clarksborough, it would be five thirty. The rehearsal was set for seven and the dinner afterward at eight thirty. Hadn't I promised my daughter I wouldn't let this investigation get in the way of her big day?

What in the world was I thinking?

25

Flower Power

The car was abuzz with energy all the way back to Clarksborough. I did my best to get my mother to calm down, but she would not be calmed. She bled me for information, which I gave at breakneck speed. We somehow made it home in time to drop off their luggage and change clothes then go on to the church for the rehearsal. I played it cool, putting my best foot forward. Tonight was all about my daughter, nothing else. No one outside of my parents and Warren needed to know about my adventures of the day, at least not yet. Folks would find out soon enough.

We had a fabulous evening together rehearsing for the big day and then celebrating afterward at Lee Yu's Garden. Candy's face beamed with joy from beginning to end. Yes, she was a Proverbs 31 woman if I ever saw one. What a fabulous life she had ahead of her. Warren and I did our best not to talk about Jim Roever's arrest in front of the kids, but as we drove home from the restaurant, I filled him in.

"I'm glad O'Henry was there, Annie," he said. "And praise God everything ended well. Sometimes I worry about you. Other times, I'm so proud of you I could bust my buttons."

I leaned over and gave him a kiss on the cheek—right there, with both of my parents in the backseat.

I slipped into bed that night, overcome with emotion.

My mind reeled backward to the events of the past three days. They all sort of merged together. The rehearsal. The investigation. The dog. My parents. The eastern hemlock tree.

Had I really tracked down Fiona's killer? That Roever was a bad seed, all right. How ironic that a tree had cracked the case wide open, especially in light of our church gardening project. I'd never given thought to flowers, plants, trees, and such, and now they consumed me. As I drifted off to sleep, visions of Pesto-Matic floated through my brain, all mixed up with images of colorful, fragrant daisies and tall, majestic eastern hemlock trees.

The next morning I awoke feeling more than a little groggy. I tried to rise from the bed but found myself somewhat frozen in place as the Lord reminded me that, even on the busiest of days, I needed to slow down. *I come to the garden alone, while the dew is still on the roses. . . .*

"Okay, Lord. I get it."

Pausing to pray, I thanked Him for walking me through the past several weeks and for returning Sasha, who now slept soundly at my side. I praised Him for the joys that lay ahead, the things I hadn't even experienced yet. *And He walks with me, and He talks with me, and He tells me I am His own. . . .*

I opened my Bible, and the Lord led me to a scripture, one I'd read dozens of times over the years but never really contemplated: "Flowers appear on the earth; the season of singing has come, the cooing of doves is heard in our land."

I pondered the words. We'd been through our

share of ups and downs over the past few months, but the flowers really had appeared on the earth. One need look no further than the courtyard of Clarksborough Community Church to see.

Were we entering into a new season? Had the time of singing really come? I chewed on this idea for a few seconds as I rested my head against the pillow. Just a few weeks ago, I'd struggled with my own mortality. Losing Fiona had almost done me in. But now. . .now I had to conclude the obvious. God had big plans for me. I could sense it. Feel it in the air.

I breathed deeply and thanked the Lord for His overwhelming presence. The sound of Warren's snores brought a certain comfort. That and the feel of two warm dachshunds pressed up against my right leg. Yes, life was certainly back to normal in the Peterson household.

Only, it wasn't. Not today, with so much to do! What was I doing lying in bed? We had a two o'clock wedding!

I sprang from under the covers like a woman possessed, which must've startled the dogs, because they started yapping like maniacs. Warren sat straight up in the bed, bug-eyed. "W—what happened?"

"It's the wedding day!" I managed to get the dogs calmed down as I added, "Get up, Warren! We've got work to do. I've got to cook brunch for the bridesmaids then head up to the church to decorate. While I'm cooking, Garrett needs your help with the. . ." I couldn't remember what it was, exactly, that Garrett needed his help with, but Warren swung his legs over the side of the bed and stood up.

"Really, Annie," he said as he ran his fingers through his graying hair, "we've got to come up with a better way to start the day."

"Oh, I just remembered!" I snapped my fingers. "Garrett and the groomsmen are setting up the tables in the courtyard at nine. That's what they need your help with. Then Sheila and Evelyn are going to meet me up there at ten thirty to decorate, after I make sure the bridesmaids get started on their brunch."

After taking a quick shower, I joined my mom in the kitchen, and we prepared the two breakfast casseroles Candy loved so much—the French toast one and the one with scrambled eggs and ham. My mother, as always, prepared grits. It just wouldn't be the same without them, she insisted. I didn't dare argue.

The girls arrived in a semipanic, and after a few minutes of making sure their plates were full, I left them in my mother's capable hands and headed off to the church, arriving at 10:35. Just five minutes after my ETA. I'd opted not to dress in wedding regalia, but in my jeans and a T-shirt that read, THE EARTH LAUGHS IN FLOWERS. It certainly lined up with the scripture the Lord had led me to this morning.

The transformation in the courtyard took my breath away. The men must've worked at lightning speed to accomplish this. Tables surrounded by a sea of white slatted chairs filled the grassy area, and the flowers framed them all, giving a beautiful picturesque quality. Several wooden and concrete benches had also been brought in to offer more seating. Off in the distance, I saw the birdbath we'd set up during our last workday. I could hardly believe it!

Evelyn appeared at my side, startling me. "How are you doing?" she asked.

"I'm shaking." I held out my hands to prove it. "Hope the nerves settle down."

"Not likely." Evelyn winked. After a bit of a pause, she said, "Oh, Annie?"

"Yes?"

"I read the news in this morning's paper. You helped the police track down Fiona's killer."

"Yikes." Had it really hit the papers already? I'd been so busy I hadn't even looked.

"So, that guy. . .the one who killed her." Evelyn's brow wrinkled. "Is that the same fellow you wanted to invite to speak to our women's group about gardening?"

I felt my cheeks turn warm as I muttered, "Well, yeah. Sorry 'bout that."

Evelyn laughed. "Just glad you figured it all out before we offered the invitation."

"Let's just chalk that up to delayed discernment on my part." I shrugged.

"Well, it's not like you haven't had other things on your mind, Annie." She gave me a pensive look. "Seriously, I don't know how you do it all. Sometimes you amaze me."

Me? Really? Sometimes I amaze you?

Her words gave me the strength I needed to dive into the tasks ahead. We all went to work at once, putting colorful tablecloths on all the large round tables. The bright white cloths would look fabulous against the color in the centerpieces and bright pink-and-orange napkins.

"Candy's going to love this," I crooned.

Maggie arrived in short order, bringing with her the flowers for the reception and the bouquets for the sanctuary. With her help, we finished putting together the centerpieces using a variety of items: wicker baskets filled with decorative fruits, terra-cotta pots with candles inside, floating candles and flowers in squatty round vases of water, watering cans filled with daisies in a host of colors, and so forth. Diedre had suggested we line the cobblestone walk with larger watering cans filled with daisies, so we took care of that, as well. All the while, Maggie and Diedre gushed over me for figuring out who'd killed Fiona.

"I just can't believe you, Annie," Maggie said with tears in her eyes.

"It's just such a God thing," Diedre echoed. "How can we ever thank you?"

"You're thanking me right now," I responded. "You're here for me. Helping. Walking me through my daughter's big day."

We ended up in a sisterly embrace.

At 11:15 Pastor Miller arrived with a beautiful water fountain, which he set up in a far corner of the garden. Behind it he placed an exquisite white trellis, which Evelyn had covered in greenery and flowers. I had no idea these items were coming, so I hardly knew how to thank her.

"You're more than welcome. We thought it would be a great place to take pictures," she explained with a wink. "And we'll leave it in the garden afterward, along with some of the benches. This whole place will be the perfect spot to pray."

I couldn't agree more. The town of Clarksborough

had once again swept in to help me with a wedding. How would I ever repay them? I started by giving Evelyn a warm hug.

By eleven thirty I'd returned to the house to shower, dress, and help the girls get ready. I was hardly prepared for the ocean of bridesmaids that greeted me with high-pitched squeals.

I slipped into my mother-of-the-bride dress—a beautiful blue number I'd found at the mall in Philly. Okay, so it was a wee bit tighter than when I'd purchased it. Couldn't exactly blame that on the dress. I'd put on a couple of pounds. Probably all that Chinese food. And the Moo-lennium Crunch ice cream. And the samples of wedding cake. Still, as I twirled around in my beautiful dress, I felt like a princess. A chubby princess, but a princess nonetheless.

Warren entered the room and gave a whistle. "You look amazing, Annie."

"Thanks, kind sir." I gave him a hug, trying not to get makeup on his tuxedo jacket. "You look pretty amazing yourself." After a moment's pause, we looked at each other. "I can't believe we're going through this again."

His eyes misted over, and for a moment I thought I might lose him to the emotion. "It's harder than they tell you it is."

"Mm-hmm." I reached up to give him a gentle kiss on the lips. "But it's more special than they tell you it is, too."

We spent a couple more quiet moments together; then Warren and Devin left the house to meet up with the guys, and I did my best to convince the girls that we needed to be on our way. Brandi did some last-minute touch-ups on Candy's hair and makeup then asked for my help in pinning on the veil. I could hardly believe it when I saw my beautiful daughter all done up. From the neck up, I mean. The rest of her, well. . . jeans and a button-down shirt weren't exactly what she'd be wearing an hour from now, but waiting to put on the wedding dress at the church did make sense.

We loaded the team of females into cars and hit the road. On the way, Candy's demeanor changed entirely. She looked a little pale. And stiff.

"You okay?" I asked.

She swallowed, and I could see the fear in her eyes as she gave a robotic nod. "I. . .I think I might be sick."

"You'll do fine." I reached over to take her hand. "Just keep your focus on Garrett. He'll keep you smiling."

"No doubt about that." She laughed. "I have it on good authority that the groomsmen are up to tricks. No telling what they'll pull during the ceremony."

"Yikes." I groaned inwardly. Garrett and Scott's friends were a little on the goofy side sometimes.

From the minute we arrived at the church, I slipped into the white zone. I saw the bridesmaids. Watched them help Candy pull on her dress. Felt the lump in my throat as I saw her in the gown, fully made-up. Vaguely remembered kissing her on the cheek and blubbering something about how proud I was. From there, through the fog, I made my way to the sanctuary to make sure Diedre and Evelyn had placed the candelabras in the correct place and that all the daisies were in their final positions. I found Maggie working in whirlwind mode.

Next I made my way out to the courtyard, where Janetta worked to put the petal-shaped wedding cake together. I whistled when I saw it, astounded. "I've never seen anything to compare," I whispered.

I took care of a few last-minute details, stunned at how quickly the time passed. At a quarter of two, I heard a familiar voice behind me.

"Annie?"

I turned to discover Michael O'Henry in a suit and tie.

"Well, don't you look nice."

"Didn't figure I should wear my uniform to your daughter's wedding."

I reached to give him a hug. "Thank you for coming."

As we walked together toward the sanctuary, O'Henry reached to take my hand and gave it a squeeze. "I just want to say how grateful I am for your help, Annie."

"Happy to be of service."

We had reached the door leading into the fellowship hall when I heard O'Henry's voice, a bit lower this time. "Oh, Annie. One more thing."

I turned back to look at him, anxious to get inside. "What's that?"

"Something Roever said when I had him in the back of the patrol car yesterday. . ."

"Oh?"

"He said, 'I would've gotten away with it if it hadn't been for that pesky woman and that dog of hers.'"

I laughed long and hard as he spoke the familiar line from *Scooby-Doo*, one of my favorite childhood television shows. So, just like Scooby and his friends,

Sasha and I had done it again. We'd solved a crime. Laid another mystery to rest. Would we ever hear the end of it?

No time to think about that right now! I needed to slip out of crime-solving gear and into my mother-of-the-bride role. With guests in their seats, bridesmaids fully done up, and boutonnieres and corsages handed out. . .I had a wedding to attend!

26

DAISY BELLE

The emotional wedding ceremony began with a slide show of Candy's and Garrett's lives. They'd chosen the background music to correspond with the timing of the pictures. From out in the foyer, I could only see if I peeked through the door leading to the sanctuary, but I saw enough to bring tears to my eyes. Was it really possible? When—and how—had my children grown up? Why, just last week they were toddlers, learning to walk. And wasn't it just a short time ago that they were stepping onto the school bus for the first time? When had they morphed into. . .brides? I brushed the tears from my eyes and forced myself to stay focused.

The music began and the candle lighters made their way up the center aisle, finally arriving at the front, where they lit the colorful candles on the two magnificent candelabras. Next came the grandmothers. My mother seemed particularly emotional today, and I couldn't blame her. Finally, the time arrived for the mothers to make their entrance.

I turned to Diedre, whose eyes filled with tears. "Are you ready?" I whispered.

"I've been waiting for this day all my life," she whispered back.

To the melody of a Vivaldi piece played by the brilliant string quartet, we were ushered up the aisle to the front of the church—carrying lit candles, no less.

When we arrived at the stage, Diedre and I placed our candles on either side of the unity candle and took our seats.

I turned back to watch the action as the flower girl and ring bearer entered, followed by the junior bridesmaid. Next to appear were the bridesmaids, with Brandi serving as the matron of honor. I couldn't help but think back to her February wedding. How different it had been from this one and yet how appropriate for her.

At this point, Pastor Miller entered from a side room with the groom and groomsmen tailing behind. I looked across the aisle at Diedre, who gazed up at her son with damp lashes.

Finally, the big moment came. When the familiar music of the "Wedding March" began, I rose from my seat and turned to watch my daughter—my little daisy—come up the aisle on her father's arm. She looked like a princess—her hair beautifully upswept with a sparkling tiara atop. Her wedding dress shimmered with each step. Even from here, I could see the moisture in my husband's eyes. How difficult this must be for him to give his daughter away.

The music ended as they arrived at the front of the church. Warren lifted Candy's veil and kissed her on the cheek. I felt a lump rise in my throat. Was it really possible? Was she really old enough to be a married woman? Must be, because Pastor Miller began the service and Warren took a seat next to me. Minutes later, Brandi sang the most beautiful love song, one that finally convinced me it was okay to let the tears flow. Warren reached into his pocket, handing me a handkerchief. I hated to blubber in front of all my friends but couldn't help it.

After the song ended, the ceremony seemed to fly by. So much time and effort had gone into preparing for it, and it seemed to end in a flash. But this was the best part of all: As Candy and Garrett shared their first kiss as a married couple, the groomsmen all reached into their jackets and pulled out scorecards: 9.0, 8.5, 10, and so on. The congregation erupted in laughter, and Candy responded by punching Garrett in the arm. Yep, she was my daughter, all right.

Afterward, as soon as photos were taken, we convened to the courtyard. The guests were already enjoying appetizers and punch. I walked from one food area to another, completely floored by everything Janetta had accomplished. She'd truly created floral masterpieces out of fruits and vegetables. And those flower-shaped sandwiches—amazing!

Off to the side of the garden, the harpist played a lovely melody, her fingers rippling across the strings in elegant fashion. I wanted to pause a moment, to pay attention. To memorize every detail. To commit it all to memory. I didn't want to forget a thing—the look on Candy's face as she became Mrs. Caine. The sound of Brandi's voice as she sang. The look in Warren's eyes as Candy and Garrett were pronounced husband and wife. The smell of the food. The colors of the flowers in the garden. I wanted to remember it all.

Sheila in particular seemed enamored with Janetta's accomplishments. I'd never seen her rave over food like this. Or consume so much of it. I secretly wondered how many minutes she stood in front of the chocolate fountain dipping pretzels, cookies, and the like.

*Better watch out, girl, or you'll end up looking like
. . .me. Hmm.*

Truly, all of Clarksborough would have to join
Diedre's aerobics class once this wedding ended.

Somehow, as the reception carried on, the news of
Jim Roever's arrest made its way through the crowd.
One by one, wedding guests stopped by to whisper,
"Great job, Annie!" in my ear. As happy as I was to
hear their praises, I didn't want anything to take the
attention away from the happy bride and groom, so
I always responded with a wink and a whispered,
"Thanks!" then directed them back to the party.

And what a party it was! The reception went on
for nearly two hours. The bride and groom cut the
cake, shared toasts, and thanked their many guests
for a wonderful day. Then, with everyone looking on,
they climbed into Garrett's overly decorated SUV. As
the vehicle pulled away, I looked back at the garden.
The tables were a mess, covered in plates filled with
scraps of food, torn napkins, spilled drinks, and more.
Was this really the same place we'd spent so much time
preparing just this morning?

Jumping into "cleanup" gear, I kicked off my shoes.
I headed to the first table and started clearing off the
trash.

"What do you think you're doing?" Janetta appeared behind me.

"Oh, I. . ."

"You're the mother of the bride. Let me do this.
The kids will help me. And Evelyn."

"I don't mind." And I didn't. Indeed, I needed to
feel needed right now.

Janetta must've sensed that. She nodded and smiled. "You know, Jake and Nikki have set a date for their wedding. It's in October. They, um. . ."

"What?"

"They want you to coordinate."

"No way." Was she serious? How could I coordinate another wedding and still keep my business afloat? Could I? Should I?

"Oh, and one more thing. Sean proposed to Maggie."

"W–what? When?"

"During the reception. Right over there." She pointed to the trellised area. "Got down on one knee and gave her the ring. They, um. . .they want you to coordinate their wedding, too. I know, because they told me so when they asked me to cater."

"Oh my." This was a fine mess I'd gotten myself into. How had I shifted from mother of the bride to wedding planner?

I walked over to the section of daisies Sheila and I had planted and stared down at the colorful petals. I wanted to find that one lone flower—the near-wilted one. Had it survived?

Sheila's voice rang out from behind me. "I can't believe you're still on your feet."

I lifted up a bare foot. "Kicked off the shoes. No one seemed to notice."

"They wouldn't have cared, anyway," she said.

For a moment, the two of us stared down at our flowers in quiet reflection.

"What happens when the winter comes?" I asked her.

"They won't last the winter." She grew silent for a moment, and for a second my thoughts shifted to

Fiona. And to Judy Blevins. Their lives had only lasted a short season, but they'd both bloomed with brilliant color and left behind a fragrance for others to enjoy.

"Will the daisies come back next spring? On their own, I mean."

"No. They're annuals. We'll have to dig them up and start over."

"That's a crime." I shuddered as the word *crime* slipped from my mouth. I didn't want to think about any more crimes. Not now. Not ever. "Could I rephrase that? I meant to say, it sounds like a lot of trouble."

"*Life* is a lot of trouble, Annie." Sheila gave me a motherly look. "It's hard work. Think of all the time we spent raising our kids. Teaching them to walk, to read, to ride a bike. Developing them into people who love the Lord, people who care for each other. It's tough, but it's worth it. And think of how many times we have to start over again. I mean, just wait. . .we'll both be grandmothers someday. Talk about beginning again."

"Sheila?"

"Yes?"

"When did you become a philosopher?"

She erupted in laughter. "I've always been one. I'm surprised you never noticed. Most of it comes out in humor, sure, but I'm always trying to make a point." She paused then turned to me with that motherly expression on her face. "And by the way, I read about Roever's arrest in the paper. Since when do I have to find out what my best friend's been up to by reading the paper? You never call. You never write. . . ."

I laughed. "Sheila, trust me. I've been a little busy." Just then Warren snuck up behind me, slipping his arms around my waist. "Congratulations, mother of the bride," he whispered in my ear.

"Congratulations to you, father of the bride," I whispered back.

We stood in silence, staring at the flowers. As the peaceful solitude took over—as the day's chaos faded behind us—I had to conclude, it had been worth it. The hard work. The planting. The preparation. Everything. This morning's scripture played back through my mind: *"Flowers appear on the earth; the season of singing has come, the cooing of doves is heard in our land."*

Sure, some flowers bloomed only once, but, oh! the beauty of watching them in all their splendor. . .if only for a moment.

27

MORNING GLORY

O ne week after the wedding, I awoke to the strangest sound. It seemed to be coming from underneath the bed.

"Warren, wake up." I poked him in the side, and he stirred. "I think Copper's up to his tricks again."

"Ugh." He pushed back the covers and sat up. I reached for the familiar lump under the blanket, hoping that Sasha would sleep through this little fiasco. She needed her rest these days.

Warren slung his legs over the side of the bed and looked around. "I don't see him anywhere."

"No way." I climbed out of bed and knelt down, looking in the usual places. From underneath the bed I heard a strange panting sound. "Um, Warren. . . ?"

"Yeah?"

"I think you need to see this." I inched my way down to my belly and gazed at Sasha, who happened to be in the throes of delivering a puppy. Make that a third puppy. There were already two curled up at her side, whimpering.

"You've got to be kidding me."

We watched in rapt awe as the third pup was delivered. Sasha, God bless her, seemed to know just what to do. And Copper. . . ? I raised up and lifted the covers on the bed, discovering him underneath, snoring. Looked like Warren and I weren't the only ones who'd slept through all the action. I crawled back down to my spot and watched Sasha clean the pup, nuzzling him with her nose and then inching him toward the others.

"I don't believe this," I whispered from my side of the bed.

"It's pretty amazing," Warren whispered back from his side.

I'd never seen puppies born before. Strange, I know, to be nearly fifty and not have witnessed something so commonplace. And yet, as I watched the panting begin again, as I watched Sasha prepare for puppy number four, I had to admit—there was nothing commonplace about it.

Minutes later, the next baby doxie arrived.

Hmm. Strike that.

After a bit of cleaning on Sasha's part, the pup looked like anything but a dachshund. It was white in color, with long wavy hair. I stared over at Warren, stunned.

"What in the world?" I whispered.

"Do you suppose that's. . . ?" He gave the pup another look. "Surely it's not the Maltese from the house behind us."

"Hmm." Yep, I'd have to conclude it was, indeed, the Maltese. I could hardly believe such a thing possible, but staring at the evidence left little doubt in my mind.

"That would explain the broken fence," Warren said with a sigh.

Within a half hour or so, Sasha had all of the pups in a row, nursing. Copper awoke and tried—emphasis on *tried*—to join her under the bed. A low growl from the back of Sasha's throat convinced him to keep his distance.

Warren offered to let Copper out, and I padded along behind them, ready for a cup of coffee. No sooner did I reach the kitchen than the phone rang. I reached for it, happy to see my oldest daughter's number on the caller ID.

"Well, good morning! You're up early."

"Mom, are you and Dad busy today?" Brandi sounded breathless, as always. She really needed to slow down, take it easy.

"We're just delivering puppies, that's all," I explained.

"No way! Have you called Candy? She and Garrett want one."

This news astounded me, especially in light of the fact that they'd only just arrived home from their honeymoon.

"I'll call her right now. Are you guys interested in some cinnamon rolls?"

"Are we ever!"

Within the hour, Brandi and Scott showed up at our front door. All the noise and confusion woke up our newly graduated son, who entered the kitchen rubbing the sleep from his eyes.

"We're parents!" I exclaimed.

"Huh?"

"Sasha had her puppies," Brandi said. "Which would technically make them *grand*parents, since they treat those dogs like children."

Seconds later, Candy and Garrett arrived. I gave my newlywed daughter a tight hug then reached for my son-in-law, who greeted me with a smile and a kiss on the cheek. Candy embraced her sister, whispering something in her ear. Then, after a couple of giggles on their part, we headed to the master bedroom to show off the new brood.

Candy led the way, doing a near-perfect swan dive under the bed. She came out with the miniature Maltese puppy in hand.

"Oh, Mom! This is the cutest thing I've ever seen."

"Humph."

"Oh, he is!" She played with the pup for a few seconds then looked up at me with curiosity in her eyes. "Do you suppose he'll have a long nose like Sasha?"

"I don't know. Might turn out to be kind of funny-looking."

"An interesting mix of breeds, to say the least," Devin threw in.

"Yeah, what would you call that, anyway?" Garrett asked. "A Mal-doxie?"

"A Dach-tese?" Scott tried.

"A Mauxie?" Warren suggested.

"A truckload of trouble." I offered my two cents' worth. Between the two breeds, there would be a lot of yapping going on. And no one's fence would be safe.

"I've got to have him." Candy looked up at her new husband with a convincing pout. "I—is it okay?"

He laughed then shook his head in defeat. "Like I would try to stop you."

Minutes later we settled into chairs around the kitchen table where I served coffee and cinnamon rolls. I noticed the interesting exchange of glances between Brandi and Scott but couldn't quite figure out what they were up to, so I came out and asked.

Brandi responded with mischief in her eyes. "Who says we're up to something?"

"I don't know. I just have the feeling there's something you're not saying."

Scott's face lit in a smile as he looked at her. "Do you want to tell them, or should I?"

At once my heart began to thump. I hated to get my hopes up, but. . .

"Mom. . ." Brandi looked at me then at her father. "Dad. You're going to be grandparents!" She laughed. "We just found out yesterday and wanted to wait till we were all together to make the announcement."

I'm not sure who screamed louder, me or Warren. I went into the white zone immediately. My ears started ringing. My throat felt dry and constricted. The room began to spin.

A grandmother?

Was I old enough to be a grandmother?

Oh, but what amazing news! I could hardly wait to see what Brandi and Scott's little one would look like.

Holy Ghost goose bumps—that's what I liked to call them, anyway—covered every square inch of my arms, and tears sprang to my eyes. In that moment, as I stared at my husband and my children, the Lord reminded me of something Diedre had said weeks ago. Something about standing on holy ground. As we all stood there together, I felt the presence of God sweep in and around us. This was truly a holy moment.

Something else occurred to me, too. After Fiona's passing, I'd been fixated on death. How like the Lord to bring a new life into the family right now to remind us that He was in control. That where one life ended, another began. That the seeds we planted in our lives grew up into beautiful gardens filled with flowers—our children, grandchildren, and so forth. As some flowers withered, others grew up in their place, keeping the garden alive with color and fragrance.

Suddenly all the teaching from the last five and a half weeks made perfect sense. I tried to keep the tears from flowing but could not. Instead, I swept my oldest daughter into my arms and tried to convey—through my nonsensical babbling—just how thrilled I was with this news.

28

CONSIDER A FIELD

Later that morning, after everyone left, I crawled back down under the bed to have another look at the pups. Noticing the tiniest one, a female, an idea occurred to me. The little darling looked just like Sasha. No doubt she would turn out to be just as ornery. But as I gazed at the precious little newborn, I knew just what I had to do.

Rising from the floor, I reached for my cell phone and punched in a number that had, only recently, become familiar.

Louise answered on the second ring with a hesitant, "Hello?"

"Louise?"

"Yes?" Her tone changed immediately. "Annie, is that you?"

"It's me. I have news."

"Oh?"

"Sasha's puppies were born this morning, and there's a little runt who looks just like her."

"Oh, Annie. . ." I could hear the catch in Louise's voice. "Are you saying. . . ?"

"She looks like a Ruby to me," I said with a giggle. "Though I must warn you, dachshunds are quite a handful."

"I know, I know." She laughed. "But they're also cuddly and sweet and give their owners lots of attention, which I need."

Yep. Knew that.

"Consider her my gift to you. But you'll have to wait several weeks before she's ready. In the meantime. . ." I drew in a deep breath, trying to work up the courage to water the seeds I'd been planting over the past several weeks. "I go to the most wonderful women's Bible study on Wednesday nights. Maggie Preston has just started attending, as well, and I know you two are friends."

"Yes, of course."

"Well, we were both wondering if you might like to join us. There are so many great women in our group, and I know you would love them all and vice versa."

"Really?" I could hear the hesitation in her voice, as if she didn't quite believe anyone would find her lovable.

"Yes. You've got to join us!"

I dove into a lengthy dissertation about the wonderful women I'd grown to love. I had Louise laughing in no time. Just wait till she got to know Sheila— outside the realm of funeral planning, anyway.

We started to end the call, but Louise interjected something. "I want to let you know something, Annie," she said. "I'm committed to getting on with my life. I did have feelings for Eddie at one time, but, well, that's behind me now. And I have to admit, Gloria's growing on me."

"Ah." I smiled. "Like a fungus?"

Louise laughed. "No. Like a friend."

Would wonders never cease! "I, um, heard about what Eddie did for Roger Kratz. O'Henry gave me the news just yesterday." Somehow Moyer had tracked down Kratz's wife's wedding ring and purchased it. "I think it's awesome that Roger has that ring back in his possession. I know it means the world to him."

"Well, the cranky old soul has proven to be pretty likable after all," Louise admitted. "I even heard Eddie and Gloria talking about inviting him to their lake house for the weekend. I know they really feel bad about what happened. . .not just to Roger, but to all of the clients whose jewels were stolen. They're working double time to get those items back."

"That's wonderful."

After a few more words, we wrapped up the call with a promise from Louise to visit the church. Afterward, I headed out to the living room to search for Warren. When I couldn't find him, I tried the backyard. Ironically, he was on his knees, digging in the dirt. Copper sat next to him, basking in the afternoon sunlight.

"Hey, Grandpa!"

Warren lifted his head long enough to offer a smile. "Hi, Grannie Annie."

"Ugh! Make that *Nana*, please. *Grannie* makes me feel like, well, my grandma." I stepped out onto the deck and closed the door behind me, watching him work for a second. "What are you up to?"

Warren wiped the sweat from his eyes then looked my way. "I, um, I've been giving some thought to planting a garden."

"Really?"

"Yeah. The church courtyard looks great, so I thought maybe. . ." He looked over at me with an impish grin. "Do you think you learned enough to teach this old dog some new tricks?"

Before I could respond, something distracted me. Sasha appeared at the sliding glass door. She pressed her black nose against it, and I could hear her whimpers from inside the house.

"Looks like someone's ready for a break from the kids," I said with a wink.

I opened the back door, and Sasha bounded into the yard to take care of business. No sooner did she finish than she wanted back in the house.

"That's right, darlin'. . ." I looked down at my anxious pup with a smile. "You get right back in there and spend all the time you can with those babies. Before you know it, they'll be grown and. . ."

"Gone." Warren and I spoke the word in unison. We looked at each other and sighed.

Before the tears could come, I meandered down the steps into the grass, where I joined Warren, dropping to my knees.

"So, you want a little help from a gardening pro?" I asked.

"Wouldn't hurt." He looked at me with a crooked grin. "If you happen to know one."

"I know several, but you're stuck with me." I eyed the ground shrewdly and allowed my mind to reel backward to the day we'd started the work on the courtyard. "You have to start by choosing a field."

"Choosing a field?"

"Well, an ideal location for the garden. Some place with just the right amount of sunlight." I pointed to the perfect spot at the back of our property. "And then you have to till the soil."

"Then what?"

"Then you do the planting. Then the watering and weeding. After that, you keep a close eye out for pests. They like to come in and undo all your hard work." I dove into a lengthy explanation and—to his credit—Warren managed to stay focused, even looked interested. "Now, before we begin this project," I explained, "there's just one thing you have to know. Sheila always says—"

"Wait." Warren interrupted me. "So we're taking our gardening advice from Sheila now?"

"Mm-hmm." I giggled. "Haven't you seen her yard? It's completely transformed. Daffodils, marigolds, azaleas, pear trees. . .you name it, she's planted it. Orin says he feels like he's living in an arboretum."

"Wow."

"Yes. So Sheila always says, 'Cultivate the garden within.'"

"Meaning?"

I gave him my most serious look. "Meaning, if you're going to plant a garden, you've got to be ready for the real work to take place. . .right here." I pointed to his heart.

Warren sighed then gave me a pensive look. "Like dealing with the fact that I'm old enough to be a grandfather?"

"Yep."

"And the fact that my wife is a local hero while I'm a lowly bank employee?"

"Puh–leeze." I punched him in the arm.

Warren reached over to draw me into his arms. As he did, Copper rose from his spot on the lawn and tried to weasel his way between us.

"You know what, Agatha Annie?" Warren whispered in my ear.

"No, what?" I giggled as I felt his breath warm against my face—Warren's, not the dog's.

"I told you once that I planned to grow old with you."

"I remember."

He sighed. "I just didn't realize that 'old' was coming so soon."

"Me, either." I gazed up into my husband's eyes—eyes filled with love. "But you know what? I think we're just rounding the corner. Headed into a new season."

"I think you're right. And I can't wait."

"Me, either." I nuzzled close and thought about all the things to come—the grandbabies, the upcoming weddings, the new friendships, the unsolved crimes, the editing work. . . . Did I have it in me to handle all those things?

Thinking about the future got me to thinking about the past. . .specifically, how much Warren and I had changed over the years. Thinking of those changes reminded me of my children and how they seemed to be transforming before my eyes. Thinking about my children reminded me that I'd soon have grandchildren—who would also grow and change over time. Thinking about my grandchildren—for whatever reason—reminded me that Warren and I still hadn't filled out those papers for the preplanned funerals we'd both agreed on. Thinking about my upcoming funeral reminded me that I still had a lot of living to do. Thinking about making the most of my life motivated me to want to get back into Diedre's aerobics class. Thinking about the aerobics class reminded me of my dimpled thighs. Thinking of my dimpled thighs got me to thinking about those brownies on Moyer's desk. Thinking about brownies made me hungry for Moo-lennium Crunch ice cream. Thinking about my favorite ice cream reminded me that I could probably burn off a lot of calories working in the new garden with Warren. And thinking of the garden reminded me of something else entirely. . .something I suddenly knew I couldn't live without.

"Warren?"

"Yes?" He looked up at me, curiosity etched in his brow.

"Before we get to work on the garden, there are a couple of things we're going to need."

"Oh?"

"Yes. You're going to have to trust me on this one, honey." I gave him a wink, joy flooding my soul. "In order for this garden to be a success, we're going to need two very important things: ergonomically designed gloves. . .and a two-horsepower tiller."

Janice Thompson, (now writing as Janice Hanna) is the author of over thirty novels and nonfiction books for the Christian market. Most of her novels are quirky, fun-loving, wedding themed stories. And why not? Over the past four years she has married off all four of her daughters! Janice is also a dog lover. Her miniature dachshunds, Sasha and Copper, make special appearances in her tales (or should it be tails?). Janice loves writing mysteries for Barbour and is particularly fond of the characters she has created in the Bridal Mayhem mystery series.

You may correspond with this author by writing:
Janice Hanna
Author Relations
PO Box 721
Uhrichsville, OH 44683

A Letter to Our Readers

Dear Reader:

In order to help us satisfy your quest for more great mystery stories, we would appreciate it if you would take a few minutes to respond to the following questions. We welcome your comments and read each form and letter we receive. When completed, please return to:

Fiction Editor
Heartsong Presents—MYSTERIES!
PO Box 721
Uhrichsville, Ohio 44683

Did you enjoy reading *Pushing Up Daisies* by Janice Hanna?

Very much! I would like to see more books like this! The one thing I particularly enjoyed about this story was:

_____

_____

_____

Moderately. I would have enjoyed it more if:

_____

_____

_____

Are you a member of the HP—MYSTERIES! Book Club?
Yes No

If no, where did you purchase this book?

_____

Please rate the following elements using a scale of 1 (poor) to 10 (superior):

___ Main character/sleuth   ___ Romance elements

___ Inspirational theme   ___ Secondary characters

___ Setting   ___ Mystery plot

How would you rate the cover design on a scale of 1 (poor) to 5 (superior)? _____

What themes/settings would you like to see in future **Heartsong Presents—MYSTERIES!** selections? _____

_____

_____

_____

Please check your age range:
- ◯ Under 18   ◯ 18–24
- ◯ 25–34   ◯ 35–45
- ◯ 46–55   ◯ Over 55

Name: _____

Occupation: _____

Address: _____

E-mail address: _____